TAMED BY AN ALIEN WARLORD

Fated Mates of the Ferlaern Warriors, Book 2

AVA ROSS

TAMED BY AN ALIEN WARLORD

Fated Mates of the Ferlaern Warriors, Book 2

Cover art by Natasha Snow Designs

Editing by JA Wren & Owl Eyes Proofs & Edits

ASIN: B0924XVKNL

❀ Created with Vellum

Foreword

A note to the reader.

If you found this book outside of Amazon,
it's likely a stolen/pirated copy.
Authors make nothing when books are pirated.
If authors are not paid for their work,
they can't afford to keep writing.

*For my mom who
always believed I could do this.*

*For my family, who puts up
"hey, let's eat this" ten minutes
before dinnertime.
And dust.*

*Special thanks to some awesome
readers who jump in and help
make my books better.
Alex, Deonne, Jenny, Joy,
Kristin, Laura, Meg, & Stephanie.*

Books by AVA

MAIL-ORDER BRIDES OF CRAKAIR

Vork

Bryk

Jorg

Kral

Wulf

Lyel

Axil, Gaje

(companion novellas)

BRIDES OF DRIEGON

Malac

Drace

Rashe

Teran

Kruze, Allor

(companion novellas)

IN LOVE WITH AN ALIEN ANTHOLOGY

Neere,

a Brides of Driegon short story

ALIEN EMBRACE ANTHOLOGY

Skoar

a Brides of Driegon novella

FATED MATES OF THE FERLAERN WARRIORS

Enticed by an Alien Warlord

Tamed by an Alien Warlord

Seduced by an Alien Warlord

Tempted by an Alien Warlord

You can find my books on Amazon.

Tamed By An Alien Warlord

He's shy and scarred and thinks no one will ever love him. She's determined to show him he's the hottest alien in the universe.

Durran: The Earthling females are settling into our clan, finding new homes high in the forest's canopy. Matches are being made, but not for me. Scarred as I am, none will ever glance my way. But one Earthling... Rayne's sweet and funny, and I want to scoop her up in my arms and kiss her until she moans my name. To protect my heart, I'll keep busy with my investigation into a new threat to our clan. Someone's harming our trees, and I need to stop them before our way of life is destroyed.

Rayne: To distract myself from my ongoing lust for Durran, I'm focusing on researching the substance poisoning the clan's trees and raising my five-year-old daughter. She's bonding with a trundier, and I'm worried she'll fly off into the sunset on the creature that pretty much looks like a giant hornet. But when Durran and I kiss, and kisses lead to other things, I'm thrown for a loop. Can a gruff alien trundier trainer and a single mom find true love on a planet far from Earth?

Tamed by an Alien Warlord is Book 2 in the Fated Mates of the Ferlaern Warriors Series. This standalone, full-length romance has on-the-page heat, aliens who look and act alien, a guaranteed happily ever after, no cheating, and no cliffhanger. Look for the series on Amazon.

Before
RAYNE

Two years ago, a disease swept across Earth, killing most of the adult men. The women on Earth mourned and tried to find a way to go on, but we were devastated. We lost not only those we loved but also our future.

We resigned ourselves to slowly dying out until a ping from outer space reached us. Aliens existed and they were eager to meet Earthlings. At first, we worried they'd attack, abduct us, or try to take over our planet. But they not only said they came in peace, but they also meant it. Treaties were formed, and technology was exchanged. The aliens revealed they'd lost their females to the same disease and proposed something eye-popping. Why not arrange matches? Geneticists checked us out and discovered we were compatible, and those who got into the growing program were given translators to help smooth the transition.

In our first adventure into space, a few groups of women traveled as mail-order brides for aliens on a planet called Crakair. When these matches were successful, new arrangements were made with a species called Driegons living deep below Crakair's surface.

Now another planet has sent us a message.

We are the Ferlaern, a noble species. Hunters, warriors, and riders of mighty, winged trundier. We are fearless and passionate.

Here is our offer: Settle on Ferlaern, and we will court you. Seduce you. Win you. When matches are made, we will provide for you and any young you might gift us.

Fearless and passionate, huh?

As a single mom with a little girl, it had been so long since I last tasted passion, I pretty much forgot what it felt like. I was intrigued by the prospect of meeting someone eager for a relationship instead of running away like my college boyfriend did when he found out I was pregnant.

My daughter wanted a daddy.

Could this be a match made…well, literally in the stars?

After taking a deep breath, I signed up for the program, as did a bunch of other women. We boarded a ship for the long journey to Ferlaern.

Each woman has her own story to tell, but this is mine…

Rayne

As setting sunlight bled across the sky in streaks of blood red and gold, I moved quickly across the forest floor, keeping my footsteps light. Though they hadn't made it clear why, I'd been told more than once by the Ferlaern warriors not to leave the canopy village without an escort. If I was caught, I could get into trouble.

But an escort? As if one of the guards had time to follow me while I examined trees.

I snorted, and a pesky fly buzzing around my head took off as if *I* were the threat.

The Ferlaern had to be overreacting.

Besides, I wouldn't be down here long. I'd get my soil samples and return to the village before it was time for me to pick up my five-year-old daughter, Missy, from her play date with a friend.

This couldn't wait.

The mighty aresk trees were dying, and I was determined to find out why. Even now, I could see a sickly yellow cast to their leaves. The smaller branches snapped at a subtle twist of my fingers instead of bending. Was this part of the tree's lifecycle? I didn't know, but I was determined to find out.

I wasn't an arborist. Back on Earth, I worked for a landscaping company. But I had an affinity for trees. They knew it, and they thrived under my touch.

A thumping sound behind me sent me spinning. My heart leaped up into my throat, and I peered around, taking in the dense vegetation encroaching on the narrow path.

When a small creature that vaguely looked like a tiny cat scooted from one side of the path to the other, my pulse slowed.

"It's nothing," I whispered. "Just an alien kitty." I turned and continued down the trail. "A cute alien kitty but not a true threat."

I hoped.

Partway through this section of the forest, I stopped beside one of the taller trees towering over me at least two-hundred-feet. If I stretched my arms out and hugged it, I'd barely span one side.

Our clan lived in the canopy of these trees. They sheltered our homes and protected us from the weather.

Us. I used the term loosely. I was an Earthling who arrived on this planet a few weeks ago to settle. The new wild west, my friend Piper called it. Our settlement in a deep valley several days flight from here hadn't lasted long after the duskhorde attacked. The damn creepy aliens had a taste for flesh and were determined to capture Earth women for breeding or supper. We escaped their attack with the help of the Ferlaern warriors who'd arrived to help us build. After most of our possessions burned, the Ferlaern brought us to where they spent their winters high in the mountains where they set us up in vacant homes. Domits, they were called, big, hollow, pear-shaped blossoms dangling from the trees. Each contained a living area and two bedrooms. No kitchen, but who wanted to cook? We all ate in a central domit. I still wasn't sure who did the cooking, but I probably needed to find out as I should take my turn with kitchen duty.

Later.

The wildest part of our living situation were the trundiers, the winged creatures Piper insisted looked like hornets (she was right). Ferlaern warriors rode them like dragons, though I'd yet to see any shoot flames. The ginormous beasts nested in the canopy as well, and right now, their young were hatching.

I ran my fingers along the tree's bark, feeling for loose areas, then stooped down to examine the soil mulched around the roots. So far, I didn't see anything unusual, but I'd just started my investigation.

Holding the short sword, I kinda, sorta borrowed from my favorite Ferlaern warrior, who might not be too happy if he found out, I left the first tree and crept closer to the specific one I needed to examine. Around me, ferns at least twice my height slow-danced in the breeze, and a plumed endla bird hopped up onto a waist-high rock and squawked at me, pissed off I walked through its territory. As if its fangs weren't enough to make me keep my distance, it expanded its tail feathers like a nightmarish peacock. Each of the feathers was tipped with a narrow blade. At least they couldn't throw them—as far as I knew.

I scooted around the angry bird but froze when I heard a subtle rustle in the woods behind me.

My lungs cut off as I looked around, but I didn't see anything except the bird hopping off the rock and scooting into the underbrush. With a frown, I huffed out a breath and continued toward the tree. As I got closer, I studied the bark and the roots partly covered with ages of dead vegetation.

"Poor baby," I said, stroking the tree.

It made a purring sound. Like really, a solid purr, which was kinda cute.

"Are you talking to me?" I whispered, gliding my fingers along the tree again. "You like this, don't you?" I've never had a tree respond to my touch before, but this was a new world with new creatures and plants. If the trees enjoyed a good pat, I was all in.

Something skittered over my sneaker, and I leaped backward, my arms flailing. My heart erupted up into my throat and for a second, I thought I'd cough it up.

The tiny cat-like creature I saw earlier on the path stood on a nearby root jutting from the soil, staring up at me. Only a little bigger than my palm, it had four legs with puffy fur, a floofy tail, and two very tall, pointy ears with tufts on the top. Its long snout wiggled like a mole's, and it skittered forward and dug its claws into the canvas of my sneakers, thankfully not slicing through.

"Who are you?" I asked it in the voice I reserved to lull babies.

It purred and tried to climb my pants.

"Oh, so you're the one who was making that sound, not the tree."

It tipped its head back and studied me before it essentially grinned, revealing long, thin fangs. A lot of things had fangs or tusks here on Ferlaern, and tusks were growing on me. Especially Durran's tusks. I kept imagining him behind me, his arms wrapped around my waist while he nipped at my shoulder with them. An impossible dream since he fled in the opposite direction whenever I came near.

Lifting the alien kitten, I held it aloft on my palm.

"What's your name, little kitty?" I asked.

Its nose wiggled, and it sniffed my palm before licking it. That tickled, and I chuckled.

Leaves rustled behind me again. Pulling the kitten close to my neck, I peered over my shoulder with fear raking down my spine.

There were many unknown creatures on Ferlaern, and I wasn't eager to meet any of them outside the kitten, but nothing moved behind me.

This reminded me I needed to get my mission over with and get back up into the canopy.

With the kitten in one hand, my bag hitched over my shoulder, and my sword held aloft, I moved around the tree, examining the bark and roots elbowing up through the moist, mulched soil.

The kitty purred and cocked its head, peering past me into the forest. Its tiny blue eyes widened, and it leaped off my hand and plopped on the ground then scurried around the side of the tree.

"Come back," I said, hurrying after it.

A tap on my spine made me shriek. I spun and thrust my sword forward.

Durran deflected it to the side with an easy swipe.

While a few of the women watched this Ferlaern warrior with frowns, I stared at him like he was a chocolate sundae with whipped cream and a cherry on top. I wanted to glide my fingertips along the history written in the scars on his face, though I doubted he'd ever let me.

He scowled. "That's my sword." He took it from my limp hand and twisted it one way then the other, examining it like he thought I hacked brush with it to purposefully dull the blade. "Where did you get it?"

"I…borrowed it." Crap, crap, crap. I was going to get in trouble now.

"Borrow implies permission." He bit out the words.

My lips thinned. "So, I extra borrowed it."

His scowl deepened, creating larger grooves in his face as the segments gave way to his scars. Made up of burnished gold, his skin gleamed dully in the sunlight. His black-as-night hair was shot through with deep purple strands, and I ached to run my fingers through it. Something else I doubt he'd allow. "There is no such thing as extra borrowing," he said.

Yeah, well, I invented the term.

"I'm sorry," I said, aiming for contrite. "I couldn't come down here without protection, and you sorta left your sword lying around."

"Where?" His thick brow knitted together.

"I, um, well, when you left it with Berrand for repairs, I adopted it."

"Swords are not tiny creatures to be adopted."

Like the kitty? I needed to find the poor thing and take it home. Missy would love it. Hell, I loved it already. Unless Durran was offering, I needed someone to snuggle up to in bed each night.

"Would you have let me borrow it if I asked?" I was truly curious about his answer. "I bet you would have stomped away without giving me an answer."

He blinked as if he didn't know how to take me. Welcome to my life, buddy. I sure didn't know how to take him.

"You can have your sword back. I'm all done with it," I said, my throat tightening as it always did when I was close to him. Like someone hit a switch, I became a mix of teenage giddy and straight-up womanly lust. "What, err, are you doing here?" I carefully tucked my bag of tools and sampling equipment behind my thighs. Because his heady scent surrounded me, making me eager to press myself against him, I leaned against the enormous tree. Actually, I supported myself against the tree. What was it about this guy? He could turn my knees to mush with one glance. I was a twenty-eight-year-old woman with a young daughter, for heaven's sake. Not a blushing virgin.

"Hunting," he answered shortly.

"No luck, huh?" My face colored the second I spoke. Way to make him feel bad about returning to the village empty-handed.

"No."

Ah, now this was the Durran I knew and, well, liked. He was big on sex appeal, small on conversation. The one time we were alone together for more than two seconds, he said nothing, just stared at me.

"Do you hunt often?" I asked to make conversation.

"Sometimes."

Hey, we were making progress, moving from simple stares to limited sentences. Within a hundred years, we might work up to complete paragraphs.

"I see," I said.

He studied my face, so I took a second to check him out, too. From the first time I met him, I was drawn to this alien, but so far, he seemed oblivious to my dubious charms. And let me tell you, I turned them on, trying to draw his attention. Short of dancing in front of him naked, I'd used the usual methods, including sidling up to him and talking about the weather. Offering to fix him a plate of food in the community dining domit. Asking him to repair my unbroken domit door—while he mumbled something I took as agreement, he'd yet to stop by to "fix" it.

He slunk away each time I spoke.

"What are you hunting?" I asked, tipping my head back to look up at him. At seven-one or two, I was eyeball level to his nicely muscled chest. The tips of his six-inch horns jutted upward through his black and purple hair, and I wanted to grab onto his horns and run my fingertips down their thick lengths. His locks hung to the middle of his back and some women might be turned off by a guy with hair longer than hers. Uh-uh. All I could picture was the strands gliding across my naked skin while he strained above me.

My skin flamed. I needed to drag my brain out of the gutter. The chance of sex between me and Durran was as possible as me becoming President of this planet and let me tell you, no one was suggesting I run for election.

"Liscards," he said abruptly. "I was about to hunt liscards."

"For dinner?"

"No one eats liscards."

"Then why hunt them?"

"We need to keep the population down so they don't eat the trundier hatchlings." His feet shifted, and I could almost picture him telling himself he was done with this conversation and me, pivoting, and running all get out in the opposite direction.

"You're the one in charge of the trundiers, right?" I asked, hoping if I focused on his job, he'd remain grounded in my vicinity.

A swallow worked its way down his throat, and his deep green eyes strayed everywhere but toward me. "I'm head trainer." His thick, husky voice sent electric tingles down my spine. The effect he had on me really wasn't fair.

Leaves crunched behind him, and something released a low, growling sound like two boulders grinding together.

I cocked my head, wondering what it might be.

Durran spun, his hand seamlessly pulling a short sword from the scabbard on his chest.

The ferns swayed and branches broke as something came near.

"Hide, Rayne," he hissed.

A giant crocodile burst from the bushes and stomped toward us with its fangs dripping goo and its claws churning up the soil.

2

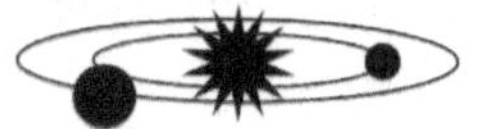

Durran

I issued a guttural challenge and bolted toward the liscard. Leaping up onto its back, I grabbed one of the numerous spine spikes and wrapped my tail around its neck. The beast's sharp, scaly sides ground against my leather pants, reminding me why we wore nearly indestructible clothing.

The furious creature reared onto its hind legs, the other eight slashing out, claws extended. It twisted and wrangled, determined to knock me off its hide.

Liscards had one vulnerable area, and they protected it with every weapon at their disposal. I'd need to work fast to get to that area before it attacked Rayne.

Rayne—beautiful Rayne—cringed against a tree before wisely slinking around the side, out of sight.

The liscard caught the movement and despite my gouging ineffectively at its back with my blade, it stomped after her.

They not only climbed our trees to eat our trundier hatchlings, but they also had a taste for flesh and weren't above attacking a Ferlacrn. A smooth-skinned, soft human would make a delightful treat.

As it galloped after her, its claws slashing the ground, I gripped my blade between my tusks and grabbed onto the creature's ruff. I leaned sideways and with my legs tight on its neck, worked my way toward its throat. My spine jarred, and my head smacked against the liscard's, jarring my teeth together. I groaned but hung on.

The liscard circled the tree.

Spying it coming her way, Rayne squawked and backed from the tree, her hands lifting. She looked for a weapon, and I regretted taking my second sword from her. I could toss it in her direction, but it wasn't clear if she knew how to use it. And a liscard could only be killed in one way.

The creature stalked Rayne, growling. Saliva dripped from its mouth, splattering the ground as it bellowed and rushed toward her.

My heart thundered, and desperation filled me. If I did nothing else in life, I would save the female I was drawn to like no other. She didn't want me; she'd never want me, but that wouldn't stop me from giving everything I could to keep her from harm.

Rayne yipped and bolted with a bag clutched in one hand and a fluffy creature in the other. The liscard grunted and took off in her direction. It would rip her to shreds if it caught her.

Not as long as the gods breathed life into my body.

Shifting, I worked my way down the creature's thick neck. While it was natural to go for its throat, steel armor covered that vulnerable area, a worthy protection. But with the right blade and the right angle, a determined warrior could defeat the liscard. We usually suspended traps from trees and when they were caught, killed them. They bred like flesers, producing twenty or thirty young in each batch, and if we didn't keep the population down, they'd overrun us. They weren't the best climbers but a few still found their way to the trundier hatchling grounds to feast.

As it lumbered after Rayne, who full-out fled, I reached the front of the creature's neck. I shot another look Rayne's way and was grateful to see her gliding behind a tree.

I grabbed my blade from my mouth. The creature stopped at the tree and sniffed to pick up Rayne's scent. It seemed to have forgotten I clung to it like a blood-sucking leete.

The liscard growled and bolted around the side of the tree. I hung on with one hand and my legs, determined not to be knocked off by its feverish passage.

Rayne yelped and raced across a small open area. The liscard gave chase, its feet thundering through the low brush. Ferns toppled and endla birds squawked and scattered, unwilling to take on the challenge.

Rayne tripped and tumbled onto the ground. Her hand scrambled on the soil, and she struggled to rise, bogged down with her bag.

While my pulse shot through my head and fear grabbed hold of me and shook me, I worked my blade beneath the armored plating coating the liscard's throat.

With a shriek of terror, Rayne got to her feet and jerked forward, half-limping, half-running. She reached another tree and darted around it with the liscard following.

I worked the blade deeper, wiggling it back and forth to drive it through the underplating.

As the liscard rounded the tree, Rayne screamed. Reeling backward, she fell, her bag flying over her head to land with a smack behind her. The fluffy creature she held scrambled into the dense brush at her side.

Muscles straining and with my heart on fire, I shoved my blade forward with all my might. It sunk to the hilt.

The liscard paused and groaned. Its head lowered, and its eyes rolled back in its head. With a huffing growl of defeat, it toppled forward.

Leaving my blade, I leaped to the side to avoid being crushed. I tumbled across the ground and rose to my feet, pulling another blade as the beast smacked onto the mulched soil with a resounding thud. A musky taint filled the air as it twitched a bit before going still.

I pivoted and ran to Rayne.

She lay on her back, completely motionless, with her eyes closed. Was she hurt?

Dropping to my knees beside her, I ran my fingers down her body, seeking injuries with exquisite desperation. My lungs raged and my pulse was on fire, but all I could think of was her wounded, dying in my arms before I had the chance to tell her I—

With a snorting huff, she pushed my hands away.

I lifted my head to find her gaze locked on mine.

"Jeez, Durran," she said. "If you wanted to grope me, you just needed to say so."

3

Rayne

Durran reeled away from me like I smacked him. "You don't want me to touch you," he half-snarled.

"I've never said that."

"It does not matter," he huffed. "I did not grope you. I was determining if you were injured." His spine stiffened as he rose and backed up a few more steps.

Would it make sense if I explained? I'd put myself out there for him for over two weeks now, but he hadn't taken the bait. Spelling it out when he wasn't interested would only set me up to be hurt. Again.

Let it go.

I held out my hand and after hesitating a second, he came forward and took it, tugging me up off the ground. I so wanted to accidentally stumble against him like women did in romance novels, but I was made of sterner stuff.

He patted my arm which was probably his way of reassuring a youngling. "Are you all right?"

"I've been better, but sure." I swiped my hair off my face and looked around, locating, and picking up my bag. My kitten took off when I fell but who could blame the poor thing? I'd rushed through the brush with it, sticks whipping us with a frenzy, and then flung it on the ground when I fell.

"What is that thing?" I asked, pointing to the beast. It might be dead, but it was still intimidating, like a ginormous croc lying on the leaves with its… I counted them. Ten feet projected into the air. Its tail extended almost the length of its body, and dark green blood oozed around Durran's blade embedded in its throat.

"A liscard." He strode over to it and yanked his sword out with a slurpy-grinding sound before wiping it clean on some leaves.

I swallowed and tried to hold onto my last meal. "I can see now why you hunt them."

He nodded. "They eat the hatchlings."

"And us? We live up there, too." My young daughter. My Missy! I left her up there. Sure, she was with Piper, but was Piper prepared to defend my daughter and her son from a ferocious creature like that?

"They don't come near the village."

"Why not? We're food like the hatchlings, right?"

He scratched the back of his neck. "We are, but we plant trillaphons everywhere and the toxin on the leaves causes the liscards intense pain when they brush against it, so they stay away."

"Then why don't you plant trillaphons near the trundiers?"

"We do, but the trundiers eat the plants." He flashed his tusks like this was some sort of inner-Ferlaern joke, and I just didn't get it. "They think it tastes spicy."

My brain shouldn't find his tusk-flashing sexy, not with a dead carcass steaming nearby. But crap, I did. He'd be sexy no matter where we were or what was going on around us.

"You were amazing," I said with a sigh. "Thank you for stopping it from eating me."

"I told you, I was hunting them. It's good to reduce the population by one."

I shivered and wrapped my arms around my waist. "How many of them do you think are around?"

He shrugged. "For now, none. Soon?" His tusks flashed again as if he anticipated the upcoming battle. "Many."

I froze and listened but didn't hear anything rushing our way. Yet. My body shook, overcome with reaction, but I guessed I was safe with Durran around. I couldn't imagine what might've happened if he hadn't been here…

Lose that thought immediately.

"What are we going to do about the body?" I nudged my shoulder toward the steaming carcass.

"Nothing."

I scrunched my nose. "Won't it rot and stink?"

Durran shrugged. "It won't be here long enough for that."

"You're saying another will come along and eat it."

"That is life." His gaze darted around, and his fingers tightened on the hilt of his weapon. I worried another croc would burst from the bushes.

"We should return to the village," he said.

"I…" Stomping my feet like a little kid, I grumbled. While I wasn't interested in attracting the attention of another liscard—hell no—I still hadn't gotten my samples. I was stubborn if nothing else.

Looking around, I realized I wasn't far from the tree I most needed to examine.

If the issue was just the bark and what I saw underneath, I could've investigated up in the canopy, but unless I studied the roots and soil, it was going to be difficult to figure out what was going on.

"You what?" he prompted.

"I'll go back to the village in a second." Pivoting, I walked around the croc and back to the big tree. With each snap in the woods, my skin crawled, but Durran acted casual, and his ease crept through my bones and relaxed me. He said we were safe for now.

He caught up and walked beside me, leaning forward to study my face. "Why not return to the village right away?"

"Before we were interrupted, you were about to tell me more about your job."

A frown filled his face. "My job? What does that have to do with anything?"

"Head trundier trainer. I imagine that's a lot of work." Each of the Ferlaern was bonded with a mature trundier, and my friend Piper's son, Noah, recently formed his own bond with a hatchling. My daughter, Missy, kept begging me to take her to the hatching grounds, but she was a child still. I wasn't ready for my little girl to hop on the back of a creature that looked like it would be just as happy eating her as giving her a ride. It would take her high in the sky on its back and she'd fall off. I just knew it.

Actually, I'd never be ready for that.

"Training is not a lot of work," he said with a frown. "Back to why you left the village and ventured to the ground alone and why you refuse to return to the canopy."

"I came down here to examine the trees." First, I needed to find the kitten before a liscard ate it. "Kitty," I called, rubbing my fingers together. "Here, kitty, kitty."

"Kitty?" His thick brow ridge furrowed. "Why do you say this?"

"Before the liscard interrupted us, I found a cute little kitty, and I want to adopt it."

"Like my sword."

"That was borrowing," I said. "This is different."

"I do not see how it is different."

"I returned your sword," I said with a lifted brow.

"And I will return it to you once it is repaired."

"Really?" I gushed. "You'll give it to me?"

"Of course, why not? I have others." He palmed his chest, from which at least ten other weapons of varying sizes projected. He wore leather straps crisscrossing his torso and shoulders, and not an inch of material was wasted.

"Will you teach me to use it? Because I'm a lover, not a fighter."

He paused on the path. "I could."

Not a full commitment, but I'd work with it.

I rushed forward, eager to get to the tree, but I slammed into someone stepping from the bushes and onto the path.

"Ah, Rayne," Crall said. A hunter, he recently asked if he could court me, but I put him off. There was only one Ferlaern I wanted to court me.

"Hi, Crall. How are you?"

His gaze scanned the area, landing on Durran coming up close behind me. "I am acceptable. What are you doing here…with him?"

The bitter accusation in his tone sent irritation shooting up my spine.

"It's really none of your business, is it?" I asked.

He stiffened. "If you accept my suit, it is. I will only accept complete obedience in a mate and speaking or walking with other males is forbidden."

Crap. He was one of those guys, huh?

His words got my back up. "I haven't accepted your suit, now have I?" If Durran wasn't listening to every word, I'd tell Crall I'd never "consider his suit" now. Why would I want to date a jerk? But I didn't want to insult him in front of Durran. Guys could be touchy no matter what the species.

I'd tell him later. ASAP later.

"Keep this in mind, female," he said. Without another word, he shouldered past us, moving deeper into the forest.

Glaring at his retreating back, I bit back my snarl and continued toward the original tree I examined.

"Crall," Durran said, stopping beside me.

"Yup, Crall."

"Do you…" He ran his fingers through his gorgeous hair. I bet it was silky. Would I ever find out?

"Nope," I said, guessing where he was going with his comments. "Not even the slightest."

Durran's back tightened. "I will speak with him, if you wish."

Crap, like a dad on the porch with a shotgun? No thanks. "It's okay. I don't imagine he'll come scratching at my door again."

He huffed and turned to the tree. "You said you wish to examine the trees. Why?"

I shrugged off my unease about Crall and focused on the poor tree. "They're sick."

His eyes widened, and his mood sobered. "What do you mean?"

"This." Turning, I pointed to the bark. "There's something wrong with the trees and I need to discover what's happening before they all die." From my bag, I pulled tweezers and the small container I brought for this purpose. While he moved in close enough that I could lean sideways and touch him, I carefully pulled away a bit of the diseased bark. "See? It's peeling."

His shoulders loosened. "It peels. We see this often."

"What about this?" A tug and a chunk of the bark broke

off, revealing the reddish stain underneath I noted during one of my walks on the bridges spanning most of the canopy in this part of the valley. "As you said, a little peeling bark isn't anything to be concerned about, but when I noted the unusual color beneath, I knew something was up."

"The color *is* unusual," he said.

"Back on Earth, I worked for a landscaping company. Though I mostly planted perennial beds and rode the steel horse…" At his frown, I continued. "A lawnmower, I mean. I also worked with the trees and studied under an expert." I pointed to the red stain. "Something is harming our trees and if we don't stop it, they could die."

"This is…unimaginable."

I nodded; my chest tight.

He leaned closer to study the area then dropped to his knees and carefully removed a small piece of bark from a different section. "Here as well. Is this tree an anomaly?"

"Unfortunately, no." I strode to another and exposed a tiny bit of the trunk, revealing more red. "I'm seeing it all over." I scraped some of the material off and placed ground bits of bark into different containers. I'd likely see the same thing under my microscope—no spore or insects causing the destruction—but it would be wise to first verify we were dealing with the same thing.

"What do you think this means?" he asked, following me to another tree with softer soil beneath.

A sound made me jolt, and I peered over my shoulder, watching as the alien kitten hopped up behind us.

Durran didn't even glance back.

When the tiny creature ran up beside my knee, I caught it and dropped it into my bag. Its purr rang out, and Durran scowled as if he thought I was making the sound.

Touch me and you might find out if I purr.

Naughty Rayne. I really was a bad girl.

"I'm not sure what the red means," I said, dragging my brain back to the conversation. "But I'm going to find out." Stooping, I pulled a small trowel from my pack and dug up a few clumps of dirt, putting them in yet another container. The kitten shifted to the side when I lowered the covered cup into my pouch. It rubbed its furry face against my hand, and I giggled. Missy was going to be all over this baby.

"Something is…" He peered around with wide eyes like fifty thousand liscards stomped our way. As he shouldered in close to me in a protective way, his weapon tightened in his hand.

I looked up at him. From this angle, he was even bigger. Stooped down, my head came to just above his knees. If a woman wanted to lick a Ferlaern's cock, she'd have to kneel on a chair.

And why the hell was I thinking about licking cocks? We were in a dangerous situation. Giant creatures could attack at any minute. I needed to finish my task immediately and get back up into the safety of the canopy.

Actually, I wasn't dreaming about licking just any old cock. Just Durran's.

My ears went hot, and my face must be a lovely shade of red. Thankfully, Durran had no idea what I was thinking. As he crouched protectively over me, peering into the underbrush, I focused on my task, digging farther around the roots to obtain another soil sample.

"What will you do with that?" he asked softly, darting a look my way as I capped the container and added it to my pouch. The kitty continued to purr. It was going to need a name.

Teddy might work as this baby was softer than any stuffed bear I'd ever held.

"I want to run a few tests for chemicals, spores, and varmints," I said.

He blinked. "Varmints?"

My snicker slipped out. "The term fits with Piper's new wild west theme. When we were traveling here, she kept calling Ferlaern the new wild west. Varmints are pests or nuisance animals that spread diseases or destroy crops. It's a word I heard in westerns."

"Westerns?"

"Back on Earth, we watched something called movies for entertainment. A western is one of many genres. Movies are a series of pictures running so fast, they recreated a story. We sat and watched them while eating buttery popcorn and guzzling lots of soda or beer."

"None of this makes sense."

But he wasn't scowling, showing I was making progress. Maybe I'd crack Durran's hard shell after all.

"I have a pad of paper in my domit. I could show you what I mean about movies." By drawing a stick figure slowly traveling across the page then fanning the pages fast so it appeared as if the figure leaped across the bottom of the pad. "If you want to come to my place once I'm done here, I'll show you."

"I'm hunting."

"For liscards, and you've done an admirable job with one already. How many were you planning to kill this evening?"

"Three or four."

I gulped. "You do this on a regular basis?" No wonder he was a mass of muscles; he wrangled crocs for evening entertainment. "I'm sure the liscards will still be here tomorrow," I added. "Come on up to my domit, and I'll not only show you a simple version of a movie, but I'll also show you what I discovered about the trees so far."

I pictured us sitting close together, our heads bent near the microscope while we discussed what could be harming the trees. Our faces would draw together… I'd look up and find him studying my lips… His tail would wind around my leg, reaching higher… He'd cup the back of my neck with his big, scarred hands, and then our mouths…

"Rayne?" he said, waving a hand in front of my face. His tail swept back and forth behind him. It had a rounded, rubbery-appearing tip. What would it feel like gliding across my skin? "Are you all right? Your skin is turning a bright color similar to the plumage of the reedish bird."

"I, um, yeah. I'm fine." Reedish bird, huh? How romantic. Sigh.

Why was dating aliens so challenging for me? My friend Piper met Garek, the warlord of our clan, on our first day here. They'd barely been introduced before they were flirting, kissing, and next thing I knew, they were sneaking off into the woods for wild sex.

I wanted all that with Durran. Was that such a horrible thing to ask?

"I'd like to see what you've learned about the trees so far." He stroked his fingers down along the tree, and I ached to feel him doing the same thing to me. "How can I help?"

"You could…" Think of something! "Carry this." I held out the trowel.

He took it and slid it into one of the sheaths on his belt. This alien was a walking arsenal, and it made him hotter than hell.

In my floundering excitement, my fingers fumbled with

a cup of dirt, and it fell on the ground. I held onto my bag only because I'd be horrified to drop Teddy.

We both stooped down to retrieve the cup, and our heads smacked together.

Horns are freakin' hard.

My forehead in pain, I tipped backward. Unbalanced, I grabbed for one of the leather straps crisscrossing Durran's chest. I smacked onto my back in the soft leaves. Carried by my momentum, Durran landed on top of me.

Holy hell.

I blinked up at him. He was so close I could lick his mouth if I lifted my head just a few inches.

He stared at my lips, and a soft groan rumbled in his chest. He was either carrying something large and solid in his pants or there was action going on below the beltline. Would it be inappropriate of me to yell yay?

"Durran," I whispered. "Earlier I said all you had to do was ask if you wanted to touch me."

"Yes," he hissed, his gaze still trained on my mouth.

I lifted my head slowly, giving him every opportunity to pull away or demand I should get up off the ground and return to my domit.

My hands glided up his bare arms to his shoulders, and I held on tight.

Then I pressed my mouth against his.

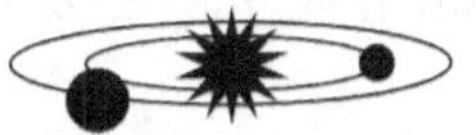

4

Durran

Rayne's lips touched mine. Was it an accident?

As I lay on top of her, struggling not to pump my hips against her, I waited to see where this was going.

Was she embarrassed or disconcerted? I couldn't tell.

I wanted to feel her colorful cheeks beneath my fingertips, but I couldn't touch her. She wouldn't welcome it.

Her fingers stroked up my neck and latched onto my horns. Fire shot through me. Horns were sensual, and it was common for a mate to hold them while her male mounted and rode her to complete satisfaction.

My cock jerked forward, begging to be buried deep within Rayne's warmth.

She moaned, and her tongue teased my lips.

This was not an accident.

Unable to hold myself back, I essentially ravaged her mouth. My tongue dipped between her lips, stroking hers. Entwining with hers.

She moaned again, and the heady sound made my bones turn to the softest mud.

I cupped her ass with my palm and lifted her up

toward me as I ground between her parted legs. Now I'd shock her. She'd been stunned when she fell on the ground. Even more stunned when I landed on top of her. Now she'd realize our lips were locked together and wrench away. She'd back up then tongue-lash me for daring to show her my need.

Her legs wrapped around my waist, and she rubbed herself against me.

Fuck.

She moaned again, and I drank the lush sound in, savoring it. I would give my very life to hear that sound each sunslice.

I softened my kiss and glided my hand up her side, pausing at the mound of her breast. My thumb boldly rubbed across her nipple, and it tightened to a savory bud. She arched her spine, and her tongue lashed against mine.

I couldn't get enough. I needed it all and I wanted it now.

Rocking against me, she whimpered and clung, her hands pumping my horns. My cock tightened further, eager to feel those fingers wrapping around its length.

I broke my mouth free from hers and kissed along her neck. Damn, she was sweeter than I ever imagined. To think she was willing to kiss and touch me. That she didn't see—

My scars.

Breaking free, I thrust up and off her. Of course she saw my scars; she only forgot about them for one munette. Scared by the liscard's attack, she wasn't thinking straight. Soon, she'd realize she didn't wish to be anywhere near me.

I turned and stomped to the tree, scooping up the cup of dirt she dropped as I passed.

I couldn't look at her, couldn't face the condemnation

I'd find in her eyes. I never should've touched her or kissed her, let alone ground my cock against her sweet body.

She sat up and the weight of her gaze hit my spine like a lash. Her sigh stretched between us, but I backed away while I renewed my resolve to avoid her.

"I see," she said softly, but did she?

Probably. My scars drew everyone's attention.

My chest tightened, and I girded myself for a sign of rejection.

She rose to her feet and retrieved her bag from the ground without making eye contact. She didn't say a thing.

I wanted her to yell at me, to tell me to leave her alone. Then I could slink behind my pride and hold onto my heart.

It might already be too late for my heart.

Her steps slower than I'd expect, she passed me, heading to a cluster of vines that would take us to the canopy.

"Coming?" she called over her shoulder as she grabbed onto one.

"Yes." It was all I could do to hold my head up as I slunk behind her. "I am sorry," I said, putting all my turbulent emotions into the words.

She didn't turn. Didn't look my way. But her hand tightened on the vine. "Are you sorry you started or sorry you stopped?"

"Stopped." I smacked my forehead. "I mean started. It was wrong."

"I see." She barked out the words through gritted teeth. See? I made her angry with my kiss. "Well, we'll have to make sure it never happens again, then, won't we?"

Exactly.

A liscard burst from the brushes, rushing our way, a welcome distraction from my growing dismay. I was tempted to remain on the ground. I could leap onto the beast and do my job.

But when Rayne's panicked gaze met mine, my heart softened to her all over again. I wrapped her up in my arms, knowing this was the one and only time it would ever happen again.

I tugged on a vine, and we shot up into the canopy.

5

Rayne

Under vine power, we flew up into the treetops. Durran kept me secure in his embrace, but it was clear he held me for nothing more than transportation.

I could've done it myself. I had more than once.

Crap, I'd ground my mouth against his and my cunt against his cock. I'd whimpered when he touched my chest. To make things worse, I'd grabbed his horns like I was about to take the best ride of my life.

Double crap, because he propelled himself up off me then made it clear it was a big mistake.

Heat flooded my face, and I was sure if he looked, he'd tell me I looked like the reedish bird again.

I flung myself at him, and he turned me down.

It hurt to be teased with a taste of someone only to have him yank it away, but I opened that fictious door and stepped through it. He didn't invite my touch, let alone my kiss.

Well, I wouldn't open that door again.

We landed on the decking, and I strode to my domit, not sure if I wanted him coming with me to look at the samples any longer. The sun was setting, and it was probably too late to see. I could invite him back in the morning if his interest were true, or let it go and handle this myself.

I needed to start patching up my wounded heart.

When he followed me, I sighed. Perhaps I did care. I wanted him inside my domit and not just to look at soil samples. I wanted to handle this mystery together, to share theories and investigate clues. And I wanted to ask him why he kissed me back then pulled away.

Even more, I ached to sit on my sofa with him and chuckle about Missy's latest production. That girl loved anything dramatic and enjoyed creating skits and acting them out for me, her audience of one.

Foolish dreams. Foolish me.

When I nudged my domit door flap to the side and stepped into my cozy living room, he remained at my heels. He said nothing, and I wondered who'd speak first.

The layout of each domit was the same. Each had a living room in the center, with a small loft bedroom above. Like the family tents I remembered from back on Earth, there was a bedroom to the left and a smaller room on the right.

Missy would remain with Piper for another hour or so, and I was supposed to retrieve her before bedtime. This was intended to give me a chance to study my samples.

Without a word, I lowered my bag on the couch and carefully tugged out my sleeping kitten.

"Poor baby," I cooed. "Were you wondering what was happening?"

Durran's wide gaze flicked back and forth between me and the creature. "You have a gressler?"

"Is that what it is?"

"She."

"Okay, she. This is Teddy." Unusual name for a girl,

but whatever. I held her up in my cupped hands. "*She* likes me." Damn my eyes for watering. It was allergies. The stale air inside my domit. Nothing to do with Durran and his big kiss rejection.

"Everyone likes you," he said softly, and his gaze met mine, his filled with overwhelming sorrow.

I was so sunk into myself and the feelings wracking my frame that I hadn't considered how he might be taking this.

"I'm sorry I kissed you," I said. "I hate that this could ruin our friendship." There. That should make him feel better. My lust was a momentary thing, something we both needed to forget about.

"I understand," he said.

"Do you?"

He shrugged. Reaching out, he carefully stroked Teddy. "I had a gressler pet when I was young."

"What did you name yours?"

"Gressly."

"That's a sweet name."

He scratched the back of his neck. "It's…boring, don't you think?"

I shrugged. "It's cute."

His eyes met mine before darting away, and I swore I saw heat there. For one second, it kinda made me think he was shy, but the guy I kissed on the forest floor had made heat boil through me like lava.

Unless…

What if he was feeling as awkward about this as I was?

If I pretended it never happened, he would, too. Then we could continue growing our friendship. I could still see him. Sap that I was, I wanted that if nothing else.

So… I wouldn't tease him. I'd watch him and see what he revealed, assuming he revealed anything.

For some reason, my sour mood fled, replaced with

caution touched with a bit of hope. Maybe there was something between us after all.

"I think it's too late to get my microscope out," I said. "It's solar-powered, and the sun has…" I waved to the slice of a window, at the tiny hint of light lingering in the sky. "If you want to come by tomorrow, we could look at the samples then."

He didn't seem to be in a hurry to flee, which was kinda nice. His fingers glided along Teddy's spine, and my gressler purred and rubbed against his hand.

"You can put Teddy on the sofa if you want. I guess I'll need to get a litter box for her."

"Litter…?"

"A place for her to go pee."

He frowned as he gently lowered her onto a cushion. "Pee in a box? Why not outside?"

"If she leaves my domit, will she come back? I don't want to restrain her if she really needs to go, but… I want a cuddly friend. Someone to snuggle with in bed at night."

His gaze shot to my room. All our domits were laid out the same. Yeah, I'd love to snuggle up to him at night but that didn't appear to be an option.

"I missed pets a lot," I added.

"If you're kind to her, she'll leave to do what she needs to, including hunt, and return to…snuggle."

"Since she's the best offer I've had in ages, I'm going to take your word for it."

He squirmed, and the last thing I wanted to do was make him feel pressured.

"What's a microscope?" he asked, changing the subject.

"You are going to be amazed," I gushed. "If I hadn't gotten pregnant in my third year of college and quit at my parents' urging to find a job and raise my daughter, I would've finished my degree in biology. I love everything science. As for the microscope, mine's an older model but it still works well. It allows you to look at things many times magnified."

"I'm not sure what you mean."

I grabbed the magnifying glass I left on a table to show him a simpler version. "This is Missy's. I'm teaching her about science. We study leaves and bark and insects with this." Handing it to him, I guided it so he could look through it at Teddy.

His gaze widened. "This is amazing."

"Isn't it?" I gushed, enjoying sharing my favorite thing in the world.

"Does Missy enjoy science, too?"

"She really does."

His probing gaze met mine. "Does her father?" He held up his hand before I could speak. "I apologize. This is nothing you need to share."

"Are you merely curious or do you truly want to know?" I watched him, hoping I'd be able to tell.

His pause went on so long, I suspected he wasn't going to answer. "I truly want to know," he finally said.

I waved to the sofa. "Sit, and I'll be happy to tell you." I dropped down onto the cushions and he joined me. Kinda had to as there weren't any other chairs. He gingerly perched on the edge of the cushion and seemed to take an inordinate amount of care to avoid brushing his leg against mine.

Jeez, I didn't have ticksies. A Missy word, but it fit.

Rather than grumble, I launched into my story. "As I said, I got pregnant during my last year of college. I never should've slept with Craig, but there was no going backward after it happened. When I found out I was going to have a baby, he essentially bolted." Kinda like how Durran was behaving, though only from a kiss. Well, and general conversation. But I had a feeling the two males were vastly different. Craig ran because he didn't want to take responsibility.

Why did Durran run?

"I could tell right away he wasn't a committing kind of guy," I said.

"If one of our females carried a Ferlaern youngling, her male would do whatever he could to be a part of the child's life," Durran said gravely. "You're saying this... Craig did not?"

"Well, he didn't exactly abandon us, but he just wasn't cut out to be a parent. He came by to see her once after she was born but refused to hold her. That sucked. At least she was too young to understand what his rejection meant."

His perceptive gaze met mine. "You understood."

My heart hurt now like it had back then. "I guess that feeling of rejection will never go away."

"I'm sorry."

"Thanks." I rubbed my finger along the seam running down the side of my pants. My eyes stung, and I couldn't meet Durran's intent gaze. Would I see sorrow or condemnation there? "Sometimes, I blame myself. If I'd been... I don't know, a better person... If I gave him what he needed, would he have stayed?" There was no swallowing the lump in my throat.

His hand reached out, palm up, and when I laid mine there, his warm fingers wrapped around and held tight. "It's hard not to blame someone else's actions on ourselves, isn't it?"

"Yeah." I sucked in a breath and shoved it back out. "At least Missy doesn't seem to notice. I mean, sure, I think she'd like someone to call dad, and maybe having a father figure around will matter more as she grows older, but she's happy with just me."

"You're an excellent mother."

"Thank you." His kind words made it easier to smile. I was a jumble of emotions, from disappointment to sadness, to a smidgen of hope that something could be salvaged between Durran and me after our failed kiss.

"What did he think of you leaving Earth with Missy?"

"I had to track him down to get him to sign the papers. I have full custody; he signed off on that right after she was born. I wanted to give him one more chance to say he wanted to be part of her life."

"What happened?"

Did he realize his thumb stroked the back of my hand? It could be a friendly gesture, but the sparks shooting up my arm and centering in my groin suggested anything but friends.

Why was I still holding onto hope?

"After he skipped out when she was born, he sent a monthly check—that's money to help raise her. But he never visited and most of the time, that was fine by me. When I offered him the papers through a courier, he signed them and sent them back right away. No note, no nothing for me or for Missy." My shoulders slumped. "I can get not wanting to be a full-time dad—maybe, but I don't understand how someone can shut the door on a chance to know your own child."

"It's wrong," he said fiercely, as if this was personal for him, but it couldn't be. His arm went around my shoulders in what I took as a brotherly hug. Maybe we could work our way to something friend-like after all.

"So that's my life story," I said, looking up at him. My sofa sank in the middle and while he might not be aware he'd shifted my way, I was. Our thighs pressed together, and his warmth sunk into me like a big hug.

"Missy and I are forming a new life here," I said. "Craig didn't want a life with us, so we left him behind."

"Us. You said us."

"Yeah." I chuckled though there was no humor in the sound. "He didn't really want me either, now did he? Oh, he wanted one thing, but he didn't truly want me for who I am inside."

"You're as beautiful inside as you are on the outside."

"Thank you. That's nice of you to say."

I came here intending to hook up with someone I could share everything with. When I met Durran, I hoped that person would be him. But it was time to let go of my dream. He made it clear he didn't want more.

"I'm not saying it solely to be nice." Rising, he paced in front of me, his boots making dull thuds on the membranous blossom floor.

"Then why are you saying it?" I asked, rising myself. I'd pace, but he was taking up all the room. Our domits might be cozy, but they were tight. While the Ferlaern brought in furniture, they mostly left the plant structure as it was originally. It already had a level floor, and the interior walls were a smooth, pale yellow. The petals at the top of the blossom lifted whenever it rained, to catch the water. This kept us nicely dry inside.

"Because you have so much to offer," he said.

Yet he refused my offer. I shouldn't feel bitter about this. Rejection was life, right?

"Any male would want you for his mate," he added, sounding so sincere, my heart was crushed. If only he wanted to be that male.

"Thank you. I'm waiting for the right guy to realize

he's the one." There, cast it out and see if he went after the bait.

"I hope he sees and gives you everything, Rayne," he said softly. "You deserve that."

While I might deserve it, it wasn't happening. And that irritated me if nothing else.

Irritation was a better emotion than despair.

As if he needed to reinforce his words with closeness, he moved over to stand in front of me. I could feel the warmth emanating from his skin. He lifted a strand of my hair and rubbed it between his fingers.

"Soft."

I said nothing, just stared up at him with heat pouring through me. If I spoke, I'd break this moment.

He dropped the band of hair and wove his fingers into the rest lying on the back of my neck. His tail joined in, teasing my spine. Leaning down near my face, he paused as if he expected me to jerk back, to put distance between us.

I stepped closer, near enough our clothing brushed together.

"Rayne," he said softly.

His lips captured mine, delicate and careful at first but with growing need.

I couldn't help myself. Pressing fully against him, I moaned as his kiss deepened. His tongue teased mine and his hands roamed down my spine, setting me aflame.

We tumbled down onto the couch together, entwined with me on top, just where I wanted to be. I ground myself against his stiff cock, riding him. If only we were naked.

Latching onto his horns, I stroked them while our kisses grew feverish.

He pumped against me, and I spread my legs wide, my

thighs on either side of his. It was just enough tease to thrust me toward the edge.

We moved together as if we wore nothing, and he was buried deep inside me.

My moans grew feverish as my body tightened. Fuck, I was going to come solely from rubbing.

His cock was a steel rod in his pants, and I wanted it filling me. Plunging so fast, I couldn't keep up.

He grunted, and his head shifted back.

Then he watched me, his eyes never leaving mine, as I ground against him.

His breathing hitched. I keened.

Reaching beneath my shirt, he stroked my breasts, rolling the nipples. I wanted to be naked, riding him while he drove himself upward, but it was too late.

My body took over, driving me against him until I crested the top of the world. I shuddered and tipping my head back, barked out a cry of satisfaction.

Spent, I collapsed on top of him.

His tail stroked my back with infinite care while his fingers wove through my hair.

When footsteps thudded on the wooden decking outside my cozy home, I jerked up, my gaze widening.

I climbed off him, and he rose. He strode to the small window near the stairs and remained there while I straightened my clothing and got control of my body.

"I'm sorry," he said softly, not turning.

Wait. What the hell?

I wanted to rail at him, to ask him what in the world was happening between us. This was no mistake; we both wanted it.

But…

If he was shy like I theorized earlier, he might have no

idea how to handle this moment. The best thing to do was see where this went. Let him lead and follow.

For now.

"Hey, no problem," I said, struggling to sound casual. The moment I said it, the tension left his shoulders and his posture eased. "These things happen."

"They do." He still didn't turn.

I wasn't sure what to make of it, but I knew one thing.

I wanted to ride Durran again. Only this time, neither of us would be wearing clothing.

6

Durran

I didn't know how to behave, how to tell Rayne what happened between us was the most wondrous, beautiful thing in the world. Instead of holding her and murmuring whatever males did after a munette like that, I fumbled my way off her sofa, raced to a window slit, and stared out. I couldn't look at her. Even worse, I apologized like it was a mistake.

Anything but. I ached to peel off her clothing and lick every bit of her body. I wanted to taste her satisfaction, suck her clit until she couldn't think of anything but me and what my mouth was doing to her.

"I have to go get Missy at Piper's," she said casually, though a hint of reserve came through in her voice. "Would you like to come by tomorrow and look at the samples with me under the microscope?"

Turning, my gaze shot to the door. The walls. Hell, even the stairs. I didn't dare look at her. What if I saw condemnation on her face?

No, what if I saw desire?

I'd never been with a female before. This… What we

did was amazing. My body ached, demanding I take more, but I didn't know how. Did a male just walk over to a female and touch her, stroke her hair and her body? Or was he supposed to woo her in some way I couldn't imagine? What if he did whatever he could dream up and she pulled back or said she… I wasn't sure what she might say. She needed time. She wanted…

What did females want?

Courtship. That's what they wanted. A tradition as old as the Ferlaern.

My spine loosened, and I started to plan. I would formally court Rayne, and I would see how she responded. I'd take cues from her words and behavior.

I'd do my best to win her.

"Durran?" she said in such a neutral tone, I wasn't sure how to respond. "The samples?"

With new hope rising inside me, I shrugged off my awkwardness and strode to the magnifying glass, picking it up. "A microscope works in the same way?"

"Yes, but better. We should be able to see if this is a chemical, a pest, or…I don't know what."

"You think something specific is causing it to happen." It was a wonder I could speak normally. All I could think of was her body over mine, grinding against my cock. Had I been too pushy? She acted like she was enjoying it. Our mouths… I wanted to tug her into my arms and kiss her again, but that wasn't in the early courtship plan. I needed to go to my domit and map this out. If I followed the courtship traditions used by Ferlaern for generations, I'd win her affection. She might even agree to be my mate.

I wanted that more than anything.

"Something or someone's damaging the trees, right?" She walked to the door, and I followed. "This is a change.

While it's common for plants to go through cycles where they die off for various reasons, this feels purposeful."

My hand froze as I lifted the door flap. "You think someone is harming the trees."

Her gaze met mine. "Yeah, I do."

A crack rang out in the forest, followed by a resounding boom. Our gazes met.

"Crap," she hissed. "A tree just fell." Tears shimmered in her eyes. "A tree died, and I think it was poisoned by someone."

We rushed outside and looked around, but the fallen tree must be in a different section of the forest.

Rayne leaned into my side, and I placed my hand on her low spine. That was acceptable, correct?

She looked up at me, and a world of sorrow filled her face. "We need to figure out who's poisoning the trees before they all die."

Someone was approaching the trundier hatchlings.

My eyes opened, and I took in the darkness, sensing I'd slept about six horas. The sun would make its appearance soon.

I lay on my fur bed in the guard's domit, listening, but the footsteps were not repeated. I must be imagining things.

As head trainer, it was my job to ensure the newborn trundiers lived long enough to bond and join the adult herd.

The duskhorde raided our trundier eggs five cycles ago. They not only decimated the season's hatchlings, but many of us were also wounded during the battle.

I was left with deep scars on my face and upper chest.

To protect the trundiers, we placed guards. Tonight, the guard who usually covered nights was sick, so I took his watch.

Shifting on the furs, I tried to get more comfortable, but I had a feeling I would not find rest again this night. When I dropped down onto the bed, I was awake for horas thinking about kissing Rayne. The only way I could distract myself from what happened with her was by speculating about what was happening with our trees. Was this part of the forest's lifecycle? If so, there seemed to be no record of it in our oral history. Today, I'd seek Narcial and ask her; she'd know if something like this occurred in our past. If so, she might know how to stop it.

Where would we live if our trees died? This was our winter home and the breeding grounds of our trundiers.

All thinking did was create more questions.

Had I imagined Rayne's response to my kiss? I must've. I was so lost in her scent the feel of her beneath me, I blocked everything else.

Fuck. Had she struggled to break free, and I missed it?

I needed to apologize for my brutish behavior. Rayne was the brightest star in the sky. The most delicate blossom in the forest. Unobtainable to someone as battle-scarred as me.

From the munette the Earthlings arrived, and I met her, I prepared myself for Rayne to lay her gaze on one of my fellow warriors, to give him all her smiles. It would hurt when she matched with someone else, but I accepted that. I wanted her happy, though I knew it would never be with me.

More footsteps dragged me from my self-recriminations. I couldn't see the person, but I sensed them walking on the decking overhead, their pace stealthy.

Rising from my low bed, I slunk from the room, not

taking time to don my boots or pants. Now that the Earthlings were part of our community, I wore a cloth of the loin, as they called it, to bed while on duty. It didn't cover much, but I was told it didn't "offend the female sensibilities," whatever that meant. They knew we did a lot of things naked, correct?

Leaving the small domit, I accessed the upper level with a vine, where I moved silently down the walkway weaving through the trundier nesting grounds.

Early sunlight slaked across the horizon, spearing through the canopy. The leaves danced in the muted light. Rayne was right. Only now did I see what she meant about the trees dying. Their leaves held a sickly pale cast I hadn't seen before. Reaching out, I bent a slender branch, and it snapped rather than moving with my pressure.

A few females warming unhatched eggs poked their heads over the sides of the nests. They huffed when they saw me. I spent so much time here, they knew me as a brother.

I sensed more than heard the footsteps ahead. Had the senior elder decided to inspect the hatchlings early? Fear spiked through me. It was too soon. I wasn't ready.

My biggest worry was for the newest hatchling, a female small for her size and weaker than the others. My belly hollowed with concern she wouldn't make it, that she would be dolced as so many others were in the past.

Preserve the strength of the herd.

Don't foster weaklings.

Excellent guidelines until they were applied to the vulnerable creature I cared for.

The little one stole my heart. Each sunslice, I fed her rich broth cooked from my own kills. I gave her the freshest water. I groomed her and told her she was going to be as big and brave as the other trundiers. But she could barely creep across the nest.

Dolcing was an ancient tradition I fought to change each cycle. So far, my wishes had been pushed aside. The elder knew best.

Not this elder.

A dull thud rang out ahead, and I picked up my pace to a near run, my footsteps light on the wooden decking. If someone intended her harm, they'd have to go through me first.

Working my way through the nesting grounds, I found nothing threatening. Each nest contained a female and either a hatchling or egg. I hadn't reached Laylee's nest, though. After her mother abandoned her, I purposefully moved her to the far end where she would avoid attention. My hope was the elder wouldn't discover her until it was too late to dolce her.

The crisp morning air glided over my segmented skin, and as I ensured each nest was secure, I suppressed a shiver. There were too few hatchlings this cycle. In past cycles, the air would ring with the chirps of newly born young, sometimes even fifty at a time. This season, only ten females conceived and fostered eggs. I couldn't imagine how our lives would change if we could no longer form bonds with our mighty winged trundier.

As I left the main nesting area and approached the little-used section where I hid Laylee, soft sounds reached me. Fuck. Someone was with her.

I ran with fire surging through my veins, pulling my short blade from its scabbard. My skin prickled as I prepared to roar into battle if I found one of the duskhorde stuffing her into a bag. Or a liscard eager to fill its belly with a defenseless hatchling.

When I reached the well-hidden nest, I left the decking

and crept up the mesh of branching supporting Laylee's haven and poked my head over the side.

My tension left me with a whoosh.

Rayne's daughter, Missy, sat with Laylee nestled on her lap, stroking the beast's still-soft wings and jutting spine. Laylee cooed and stared up at the child as if she were the most precious being in the world.

Truly, Missy was. How could a father not wish to be everything for this youngling?

I must've made a sound, because Missy shot a wild look my way. Her mouth formed a big circle.

"You should not be here, youngling," I said gruffly. Keeping my movements nonthreatening, I slid my blade back into its scabbard and eased fully into the nest to sit on the opposite side of Missy.

Laylee chirped in welcome but didn't make an attempt to leave Missy and come to me. Normally, she'd hobble to my feet and beg for attention.

Missy's face pinkened, an Earthling gesture, much like Rayne. I heard it meant excitement or embarrassment. For her, I assumed she felt the latter. A Ferlaern's segmented skin did not change color at will and when I first saw Rayne turn this very shade of pink, I thought I did something wrong. We'd gone for water together and when she changed color, I assumed this was her way of camouflaging herself from me. Essentially hiding because my face was so ugly. With embarrassment surging through me, I turned and bolted from her, though I circled around to ensure she was safe until she left the woods and returned to the others.

I teased Rayne yesterday when I told her she looked like a reedish bird because I savored watching more color light up her face.

It was wrong of me to tease her, just like it was wrong that I kissed her.

Missy carefully set Laylee behind her and stood. She hefted a stick and poked it toward me.

"Don't hurt her," she said in challenge. "You come near her, and I'll whack you. I mean it!"

"Why do you think I'll hurt her?" I asked, lowering my voice to the softest tone I could push through my sleep-roughened throat. "It's my job to care for the trundier and their hatchlings. I would never harm one."

Her pointed chin lifted, reminding me so much of Rayne, it made my chest ache. With defiance darkening her gaze, she met my eyes with steel, though her body trembled. "I heard the old mean Ferlaern saying he was going to get rid of the runt."

Our esteemed elder, Horesk, knew about Laylee already? I did my best to hide my shock from the child. I should've known even the hunched elder would sense her weakness and track her down. Part of his duties included inspecting the hatchlings a moon after they emerged from their shells and deciding who should be dolced.

To keep the herd strong, we must wean out the frailest hatchlings. I heard these words so many times while growing up, they were a litany in my mind. Despite my attempts to eliminate the practice, it was reinforced as I trained for this position.

The elder took his dolcing duty seriously.

"When did you hear this?" I asked Missy carefully, not revealing the anxiety pouring through me.

"Yesterday."

One sunslice from today, then. My heart sank. I felt useless to help my tiny trundier friend.

"I know what a runt is because my best friend had a puppy back home who was the runt of the litter. They woulda killed him!" Missy's voice faded. "They woulda killed him, and he was the bestest dog ever."

"I don't want to kill Laylee," I said, leaning back against the nest.

"Laylee?"

"My name for her."

Missy gave me a soft smile. "I like it." She stooped to stroke the trundier's head. "Laylee." When she saw I wasn't poised to leap forward and harm the trundier, she sat and tugged the small beast on her lap again. "The mean guy wants to kill her. He said so."

Horesk was a traditionalist, and rules were very important to him. I knew from the moment I first saw Laylee what he'd do.

When Laylee looked up at me with her soft, dark eyes, my soul cracked.

"How did you know she was here?" I asked. Foolish to think this remote nest was any safer than the others. Missy found her. Horesk would track her down, too.

"Laylee called to me when I was here with Noah, Garek, and Piper. I followed the sound."

Noah, Piper's son, recently formed our first human-trundier bond. We hadn't known it was possible, but Piper's youngling son not only felt the surge in his spine, but he also displayed the wrist marking showing he was the hatchling's true master. Already, he'd begun the long training period where he would work with his trundier until it responded to his commands and their bond was unbreakable. In a few cycles, they'd take their first flight together.

Everyone asked, was Earthling-trundier bonds a fluke or our new future? Only time would tell but it was clear things were changing due to the settler's presence. Much to Horesk's dismay. No one thought an Earthling female could form a maelstrom bond with one of our males, yet Piper was fully mated with our clan warlord, Garek.

Their shared mark blazed on their shoulders for the world to see. Horesk tried to rip them apart, insisting a warlord could not maintain a maelstrom bond, that it would interfere with his ability to do his duties for the clan, but the other elders changed the rules. No longer were maelstrom bonds forbidden to warlords.

Many suggested Horesk would not permit the Earthlings to bend our traditions further.

"I've been coming here the last few nights to see Laylee," Missy said, stroking the trundier's spine. "She's special."

It warmed me that she could feel what I did for the tiny hatchling.

"How did you know Laylee was a she?" Few could tell the sex of a trundier yet here was this small human being declaring it as if she sensed it.

"It's obvious." Her face tightened with indignation. "She's not a he."

I shook off my amazement though I wondered: could this Earthling become an apprentice trundier trainer? No one worked with me yet, though each youngling took a turn helping with the hatchlings to see if they contained the potential. "Does your mother know you come here?"

Rayne. I ached to get close to her, but she was no nearer to me than our two moons above.

"Mommy kinda knows," Missy said, her head lowering and the curtain of her brown hair shielding her eyes.

"She does, huh?"

"Well, um…" Her lips twitched. "I'm gonna tell her."

"You should."

I worried about this child. Our domits were secure. Guards circled the perimeter, watching for the duskhorde, though they had not been seen in this area for more than a moon. And we planted trillaphons everywhere to repel the liscards. Still, it was never safe to wander the canopy at night, especially for a small Earthling.

As Missy stroked her, Laylee's wings fluttered before resettling. I was proud to see new strength in the movement. Maybe by the time the elder tried to dolce her, she'd appear as strong as the others.

"Your… If your Mommy wakes and finds you gone, she'll be frightened," I said.

Missy shrugged.

I lifted one brow. "You think she won't be scared if she finds you missing?"

Her sigh bled out. "Maybe." She curled around the trundier as if she'd protect her from everything that might harm her. I sensed an ally in this child, a kindred spirit. "I just can't leave her. You know?"

I did know.

"She needs me," Missy said. She rested her chin on Laylee's head. "She's pretty, isn't she?"

This trundier was not the most attractive hatchling I'd ever seen, but she had something special about her even I couldn't resist.

Taking a small stick, Missy dragged it across the bottom of the nest. Laylee pounced, snatching the twig up in her tiny teeth. The soft wood snapped, and she tapped her front feet on the pieces, playing.

"Ah, Missy," a soft voice said behind us. "There you are."

I didn't need to turn. My segmented skin heated, telling me who peered over the nest's edge.

Rayne.

7

Rayne

I almost had a heart attack when I found Missy's bed empty.

Anxiety spiked through me, making my hands shake.

Teddy followed me around the domit while I looked for her but didn't find my daughter.

After Noah was stolen by one of the Ferlaern not long ago, I thought the worst about my Missy. I feared the worst-case scenarios that could involve Missy. Shutting the kitten inside, I left my domit and raced along the wooden walkways, softly crying her name. She was only five, just a baby. My only baby. Please, let her be okay.

As I crossed a platform, I slammed into someone. Hands gripped my arms, tightening to the point of pain.

"Rayne," Crall said, looking down with a flash of his tusks. "It's early, but I was about to scratch on your door and see if you wished to go to breakfast with—"

"Not now," I half-shrieked. I wrenched away from him and bolted.

"Rayne. Come back!" The weight of his stare was

heavier than a lead ball around my ankle in deep water, but I kept going.

With the hem of my nightie flapping around my thighs and my bare feet smacking on the decking, I ran across the outer walkways, peering over the railings with fear's tight grip on my throat. I expected to find my child lying broken on the forest floor below, but there was not a trace of her to be found.

It was only when I remembered Missy going on about one of the hatchlings that I took a chance and snuck into the nesting grounds. Low voices called me to this area.

I stepped over the side of the nest and moved around Durran to stand over my daughter.

"You, you…" I said to her, my hands going to my hips. My chest deflated, and I wanted to cry.

Missy said nothing, and she didn't meet my eye. She stroked the trundier hatchling, her movement almost feverish.

I slumped against the side of the nest. With my worry gone for the moment, I couldn't keep my gaze from Durran's nearly naked body. He wore only a scrap of cloth around his waist and between his legs, leaving a broad expanse of tight abs and muscled chest for me to view. The width of his shoulders…

I needed to stop staring. Despite our kiss and hasty grinding session, he wasn't interested in me; he made that clear on more than one occasion.

Put him from your mind!

My skin tingled, like it did whenever he was near, but I needed to ignore the feeling.

I turned away from him, dragged my attention back to Missy, and I stiffened my spine. "Why are you not in your bed? I was scared. I woke up and you were gone!" The break in my voice gave away the terror I just lived through.

"I worried you were…" I shook my head, and my long hair tickled my spine. "I was afraid something horrible happened to you."

"I'm sorry," Missy said, hanging her head. "I just wanted to be with Laylee."

"I assume Laylee is the name of this trundier pup?"

"Yup."

I could almost feel Durran's intent gaze focused on my bare legs. The nightgown barely covered my butt cheeks. Unlike Crall, his stare made my blood simmer with excitement.

But…

His rejection yesterday still stung. If he wasn't interested, why bother looking?

Gawk all you want. I wasn't going to take time to find my robe when my child was missing. I wore undies. My nightgown covered the important areas. I wasn't nearly naked like him.

Do not stare at his gorgeous body.

"Laylee needed me, so I had to come," Missy said, returning my attention to her, where it needed to remain. But I could almost taste his heady scent in the air. It sunk into me and warmed me to my very core.

"In the middle of the night?" I asked.

"I wasn't sure you'd let me come during the day, Mommy."

"Not alone, but you've been here with Noah and Piper. You shouldn't come here when…" I couldn't mention the liscards. While my daughter needed to understand that she couldn't just sneak out at night alone, I didn't want to frighten her more than necessary. As long as she obeyed me and came here with others, she'd remain safe and oblivious to the larger threat.

"I was on guard tonight," Durran said. "She is safe."

"I'm sorry, Mommy," Missy said, her gaze shooting between me and Durran. She sensed I was unsettled about him, but she didn't know why.

Frustration poured through me and not solely because of my daughter's actions. I sunk down beside her and leaned against the side of the nest, stretching my legs out in front of me. "From now on, you don't come here at night. If you want to visit the trundiers, you ask someone to take you. Is that clear?"

She huffed out a long sigh. "Yes, Mommy."

Compliant for now. We'd see how long that lasted. I'd have to watch her closely. Could I set up a bell or something that would wake me if she tried to sneak out again at night?

"You need to listen to your mother," Durran said gruffly. "And if you want to visit with Laylee, I can bring you."

"Really?" Missy gushed, almost wiggling like a puppy.

I'd need to speak with her later. While Durran would make a great friend, I wouldn't want her thinking he'd step into a daddy role.

"If your mother gives permission," Durran said sternly. His twinkling gaze met mine as if we were co-conspirators hatching a plan.

"Please, Mommy?"

I wouldn't deny my daughter something she loved, and it was clear she cared for this hatchling. "Yes, you can come here with Durran as long as you promise never to sneak out at night."

Her shoulders curled forward slightly before she straightened. "Okay. I won't sneak out at night." Her eager gaze shot to Durran. "Can I spend all of my days here?"

"You cannot."

"Why?" she whined.

"Because the trundiers need to rest. Any good trundier trainer knows that."

"Trainer?" Missy latched onto the word. "Can I be a trainer? I could work with Laylee."

Noah bonded with a trundier hatchling. Was that what was happening with my daughter? I'd ask Durran later, not in front of Missy who'd jump all over the idea.

"We do take on apprentice trainers, but the program is rigorous," he said.

His gaze did not caress me. His soft groan did not make my skin tingle when our legs brushed together.

Missy's face scrunched. "What's rigor…"

"Rigorous means difficult. Challenging," I said.

"Oh. I can do this…rigor thing," Missy said. Her head tilted. "But what's an appen…tiss?"

"An apprentice is a youngling learning the skills needed to be a master trundier trainer," Durran said. "A few are chosen each generation."

"Can I be an apprentice? Can I?"

"This isn't for us to decide," I said, cautioning my daughter. I hated seeing her get her hopes up about something like this. A position like that was coveted. A Ferlaern youth would be chosen instead. "I'll talk to Durran about it later." I stroked my daughter's hair and hoped I'd find a way to soften the blow if her wish was turned down.

"I will discuss this with your mother later," Durran said. He rose to his feet, towering over me. "I'm sorry. I…" His throat moved with his swallow.

"You what?" I asked, looking up, up, up to his face. I tried not to let my gaze linger on his groin. The skimpy cloth didn't hide a damn thing, and his sizeable bulge shifted. Gulping, I dragged my attention across his washboard eighteen-pack, his broad chest and shoulders with their fine network of scars, and to his equally fissured face.

With the soft morning light outlining his bronze body, he rivaled a god.

We all carried scars either inside or out, and his didn't bother me a bit. His just blazed stronger for the world to see.

"I mean I'm sorry, but I need to leave," he said.

"Why?" I wasn't trying to be ornery; I just hated that whenever I came near, he left. Was I that hideous to look at? Maybe it was my personality. I did have a mouth on me, and I never hesitated to use it.

Or the fact that I kissed him and ground my body against his, something I never should've done.

"I must hunt for Laylee," he said.

My skin prickled with embarrassment. Maybe he only liked quiet women. Softer women. Ones who didn't leap all over him.

"Laylee and me are best friends," Missy said, thankfully dragging my attention away from my churning emotions. When was I going to convince my heart, he wasn't interested? Missy stroked the tiny trundier. "We're gonna be friends forever. I'll visit her with Durran, and I'll train her."

"I'm glad you've found a friend, honey," I said. "But I'm not sure things are going to work out like you believe." I looked to Durran for confirmation.

"She is welcome to—"

"I assume you're here to dolce this hatchling, Durran," someone called out in a scratchy voice from the walkway below.

Durran's body tightened, and his worried gaze shot to Missy and Laylee. "It's too early. She has a moon more before we need to consider anything like that."

"A moon will not make a difference," the elder said. "Get it over with now."

"Don't let him hurt Laylee, Mommy," Missy wailed, clutching the hatchling to her chest. The creature squawked as if it sensed the looming threat.

Horesk, the crotchety elder of the Suthen Clan clambered up over the side of the nest.

As he and Durran towered over me, I got to my feet. Not that this put me at eye level. Both males were almost two feet taller than me, even the slightly hunched, older guy.

"What's he talking about?" I asked, stepping between Horesk and Missy to cut off his glare. My daughter got to her feet and backed to the edge of the nest, the small trundier snug in her arms.

"He's gonna kill Laylee," Missy said, looking ready to bolt. She darted past Horesk, but he latched onto her arm and dragged her close while bending down to put his snarling face close to hers.

"Release the pup," he snapped, his crochety body hovering over her like an oily shadow. "I will take care of it."

"No! You're not gonna hurt her." Missy wrenched free and leaped from the nest, onto the branch leading to the walkway.

I clutched the side and watched as she scrambled down the branch and fled along the boardwalk toward the main village with the creature clutched in her arms. If I knew my daughter, I'd find her hiding in her room, her body curled around the hatchling. Missy had a tender heart, taking in every wounded creature she found in the neighborhood.

But while I also had a tender heart at times, I was a feral beast when my daughter was threatened. Turning, I snapped my teeth. I had to veer around Durran who'd pulled his blade and looked ready to skewer Horesk. I stomped so close to the elder, he shuddered and took a step backward, nearly tumbling over the back end of the nest.

"Leave my daughter alone." Each of my words was punctuated with a poke in his belly. "Do not touch her again, or I'll rip you apart."

"You do not threaten me, Earthling female." Disgust twisted his face, and he smacked my hand away. "This is why I do not welcome you and your kind here. You will ruin our traditions. If you wish to remain with our clan, learn your place." He shoved me, and I stumbled backward.

Durran's growl ripped through the air, making Horesk freeze. His body bristling, he stepped between me and Horesk. "Touch Rayne again, and you will feel my wrath."

"I expect you to do your job, trainer," Horesk said, his tail spiking out behind him and his horns bristling. "Do not intervene in mine."

"The pup is doing well. She doesn't need to be dolced."

"What does dolcing mean?" I asked, looking between them. I didn't like where my thoughts were taking me.

Durran's body shook with suppressed fury, and Horesk's face strangely softened for one moment before tightening again. There was more going on here than Horesk asserting his authority over me and Missy, more than just Horesk showing dominance as a clan elder, but what was it?

"The pup is weak," Horesk said, stiffening. "We need a strong fleet to hold back the duskhorde."

I was as wary as any of us about the duskhorde. Our first night on this planet, the hairy, lizard-like creatures attacked our camp in the lower valley, intent on capturing Earth women for breeding. If Durran and his friends hadn't been there, we would be lying beneath them right now.

"I will take care of the trundier hatchling," Durran bit out, his hand tightening on the short sword at his side. "Not you. It is my role as head trainer." Would this come to blows? Horesk didn't stand a chance against a hardened warrior. He wasn't even armed.

I laid a restraining hand on Durran's arm, and his scarred skin twitched. Did he dislike me so much he couldn't stand for me touching him? Pulling my hand back, I held it against my chest, over my heart that stung all over again.

"That is the problem," Horesk blustered. "You are not taking care of it."

"What is he asking you to do with the trundier pup?" I asked.

"Any decent trainer would dolce the pup," Horesk said, pushing past us and stepping over the side of the nest. He turned back to glare. "I will ensure it happens myself."

He left, scrambling down the branch and onto the walkway.

As his stomping footsteps faded, Durran sighed.

"He wants you do to something to the hatchling, doesn't he?" I asked. "What does dolcing mean?"

When his gaze met mine, the sorrow and grief there hit me like a kick in the spine.

He dragged his hands across his head, scattering his deep black hair shot through with purple. "Over the past cycles, fewer hatchlings have been born. Each is precious. But when one isn't growing as it should, we're expected to remove it from the nest, freeing the space for another egg."

I waved my hand out. "There are lots of empty nests here already. You don't need a free one, do you?"

"Horesk's opinion is what matters to the rest of the

elders." He indicated for me to go ahead of him, and I climbed over the side of the nest and slid down the smooth bark, my bare feet landing solidly on the wooden decking.

My nightgown hiked up. I wore undies, but they were the skimpy kind, something my grannie wouldn't be caught dead in. With heat flaming in my cheeks, I yanked the material back down over my hips.

Durran's wide eyes were focused on my ass.

It was nothing. He probably hadn't seen a half-naked female in a long time; nothing else.

"Sorry," I said.

He swallowed deeply.

"I'll walk with you to your domit," he said.

We reached the walkway and walked in that direction.

I looked up at him. "Tell me what the dolcing is?"

"If Laylee is not deemed strong enough, Horesk will toss her from the nest."

"Toss her where?" My skin crawled as it sank in. I knew. He didn't need to name it. "He wants to kill her."

His face pensive, he nodded.

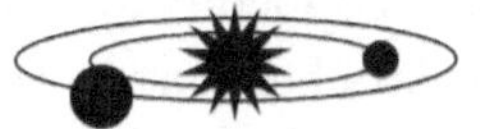

8

Durran

"I know you won't do it," Rayne said, bolting ahead of me. "But I won't let him do it, either."

"I will not let anyone harm her," I called after the female who was more addictive than an entrailire flower whose scent lulled a person close. Once they dropped beneath the plant, they couldn't get away; they'd lie there until the sticky sweet essence overwhelmed their brain.

Rayne did the same, overwhelming me with her beauty, her scent, and the sweet way she looked at me.

Her steps slowed and she turned, waiting for me to catch up. "What are you going to do?"

"Horesk will do as he pleases. I've spoken to the elders in the past, but they will not relent. Horesk controls the trundiers while they oversee other parts of our life. I have little power here, but my bonded mount, Jorlorn, and I will take Laylee to a place where she'd have a chance to grow safely. I won't come back until… Well, I probably won't ever come back because I know Horesk. He won't relent."

"Durran." Her shoulders drooped. "Don't…" Her pace slowed, and she stared down at the decking.

Sunlight shone from behind her, lighting her up like the rarest jewel and filtering through her short gown, outlining her lush curves.

My cock tightened, the culier strands elongating. My tail coiled around but stopped before reaching her ankle. I ached to touch her, kiss her, taste her. Bury myself deep inside her.

Turning, her gaze wandered down my front, stopping at my bulging groin, and when they lifted to meet mine, attraction sparked in her eyes.

"Don't what?" I asked. Some wild, unknown part of me made my hand lift. I caught a band of her hair drifting away from her head, carried by the wind. It was softer than I thought it would be. I wanted to lean against her and find out how it smelled. In my mind, it would be sweet, as tempting as the rest of Rayne.

"I don't want you to leave," she said, her chin lifting.

That…stunned me. I dropped her hair, and my hand landed on her shoulder. If I glided it down her arm, I could taste her skin with my fingers. It would never be enough, but I'd savor each munette.

I was a gruff, unrefined trundier trainer. She was the two moons and the stars. She'd never look at a scarred warrior like me.

No matter how many times I repeated the words, I wasn't sure I still believed them.

"Why don't you want me to leave?" I watched her and the world collapsing around us wouldn't keep me from waiting for her answer.

"Do you want me to spell it out for you?" Her voice tightened. "I'm stupid. I shouldn't…" She cupped her face and rubbed before her hands dropped to her sides.

"Why does it matter to you if I leave?" I pressed.

"Don't you know?"

"I don't. I—"

A sharp cry cut through the dawn, coming from my right.

"Missy," Rayne said, her panicked gaze meeting mine. She rushed across the narrow bridge to the small, covered platform on the other side.

I followed, anger rising inside me like a hive of bizzire poked with a stick.

Horesk stood over Missy, who sat with Laylee held tight against her chest.

"Leave her alone," Missy cried, trying to shield the pup with her body.

As I drew close, Rayne grabbed Horesk's arm to pull him away from her daughter, but he ripped loose and snarled at her, his tusks gnashing.

I barreled over and pushed between them—pushed Horesk hard against the rail.

My heart roared, shouting for me to eliminate him as a threat, but killing an elder would see me following him quickly to the grave.

"This female dared touch me," he bellowed, grabbing Rayne's arms, and shaking her. "I will call the council. You will be expelled with her—all of them—from the clan!"

Rayne's eyes widened, and she reeled around to hover over her daughter.

"Direct your anger at me, as you always do," I bit out. "Leave Rayne and her daughter out of it."

"She touched me." His eyes flashed fire and his hands lifted, his fingers forming claws.

I stepped forward before he could descend on Rayne again. My hand hovered on the hilt of my blade. "She defended her youngling. That's what I'll tell the council."

Horesk sputtered but he visibly wilted. "I demand an apology."

"Sorry," Rayne snapped. "Leave my daughter alone or you'll find out what it's like to stir a mother bear's anger."

"The trundier hatchling needs to be dolced," Horesk said. "Give it to me and I will carry out what needs to be done."

"You will not dolce her," I said.

"Mommy," Missy cried. "The mean man's gonna hurt her."

Rayne dropped down beside her daughter and curled her arms around both her and the trundier pup. Fury blazed in the gaze she sent Horesk's way. "My protection extends to the hatchling."

"This is not your business, female," Horesk said. "Just like the other one, you make demands. You toy with our traditions, and it will see this clan ruined." His arms lifted. "Watch and see."

"I will take care of this myself," I said sharply. "Training is my job, and you will leave me to it."

He stomped close to me, his face twitching. "And it is my job to decide who will be dolced." His finger pointed toward Missy. "That trundier hatchling should've been dolced sunslices ago."

"You're not gonna do it. I won't let you." Missy stormed to her feet, and I thought for a munette she'd attack Horesk. But she darted around us and raced toward her domit with her mother rushing behind her.

My sigh bled out, my anger turning to sorrow. I hated seeing the child sad, and it hurt to think I could lose Laylee. "Why won't you make an effort with the Earthlings?"

"They should not be here." Horesk leaned back against the railing and studied me. "They should've been left in the valley."

"The duskhorde would capture and rape them."

He shrugged. "Then so be it."

I started toward him, my hands fisting, but he turned away and strode across the bridge before I could reach him. "I have work to do. So do you, youngling."

My fury sparked anew. "You don't get to call me that."

He paused on the bridge spanning two platforms. "I can call you whatever I choose."

"You do not have that right," I hissed.

"If I don't, then who does?"

He stomped away before I could challenge him further.

With a heavy heart, I took off after Rayne and Missy, finding them sitting on the bench along one side of a platform near their domit. Missy sat on Rayne's lap, and she stroked her daughter's hair while Missy snuggled Laylee.

"The mean guy wants to hurt her," Missy said, her voice broken.

I dropped down beside them, wishing there were some way I could help the child feel better.

Laylee cooed and nuzzled my hand when I ran my fingertip across her spiny head. She nestled against Missy as if she could comfort the little girl.

"We can't let him do it, Mommy," Missy said.

"We won't, honey," Rayne said, weaving her fingers through her daughter's head. Her sad gaze met mine, and I wanted to tell her I'd handle this, that there was no way Horesk would cull the hatchling. But he was the one with power where I…had none. Not in this clan, where it truly mattered.

"I will protect her," I said. I'd find a way.

"See?" Rayne said, struggling to sound confident. "Durran will keep Laylee safe."

How, I didn't know, but I would do it. There had to be a way.

"Can you?" Missy looked up at me with tears streaking down her face. "Will she have a chance to grow?"

I couldn't promise this, not without leaving, and Rayne…wanted me to stay, even if I didn't know why.

"Is there a way to convince Horesk to let her live?" Rayne asked me.

"If she's strong enough, no one will allow him to dolce her."

"You said there are fewer hatchlings each cycle. While your tradition may say the weak ones need to…" She shuddered. "But if you don't have many, isn't each one precious?"

"They are all precious. Dolcing is done early, before a bond is formed with a Ferlaern. Laylee is still unbonded."

"What difference does that make?" Rayne asked.

"Even Horesk would hesitate to dolce a bonded trundier. But she's too young. Normally, trundiers don't form a bond until they're a few moons old."

Rayne looked up at me with a world of hope in her eyes. "When will she be old enough?"

"She still has a moon of growth needed."

"While he seems like a complete asshole, is there any way to persuade him to give her a little more time?"

"I'll ask him." Plead with him. I never had, but I would if he granted me this one thing. After all these years, after what he did to me, he owed me *something*. This would be my demand.

When Missy looked up at me with her soft eyes, I'd give her anything. What would it be like to call this youngling daughter?

So wrong of me to wonder. Another warrior would claim this family as their own, not me.

"I won't let any harm come to her," I promised, wondering how I'd keep my vow.

"We could go to Garek," Rayne said. "He has a heart, something Horesk lacks."

She was correct about that. I wasn't sure Horesk ever had a heart but if he did, it had shriveled since my mother died.

"Garek should be a last option," I said. "He's busy with the clan and shouldn't be pulled away for something like this. Horesk will remind him this is traditionally the senior elder's decision, not that of our warlord."

"A month is a long time." Rayne's back tightened. "We need to hide her then get her strong enough to please Horesk. Then he won't have a choice."

"We?" I plucked that word from her statement and held it close.

She lifted one eyebrow. "I'm going to help make it happen, Durran. For Missy and for you."

9

Rayne

"Tell me what we need to do," I said. After my past experience, it wasn't easy to trust anyone. I learned quickly how to handle everything myself.

But I trusted Durran. Assuming he could convince the nasty geezer to give us time, we could fatten the trundier baby up and get her strong enough to meet his approval.

When he threatened Missy, me, and the pup, I wanted to kick him, but I held myself back. He was a respected elder. He had power. If I angered him, he'd seek revenge.

"Yeah, Durran, what do we need to do?" Missy cuddled into my side; the tiny, winged creature nestled in her arms.

"I assume she needs to eat and do strength training," I said.

Durran looked between us, and his gaze softened. "You'll help me?"

Why did he sound surprised?

"Maybe it's stubborn of me, but I'm determined to prove Horesk wrong," I said. "Laylee is worth saving. Missy loves this creature and that's enough for me."

The trundier looked up at me and chirped. For a baby hornet-bird, it was kinda cute. I stroked its tiny head and it cooed.

"See?" Missy said. "She likes you. We need to take her into our domit. She'll be happy there. She can sleep in my bed with me and go to the dining domit with us and eat lots of food, and I'm gonna work with her and teach her to fly."

"That sounds like a lot of work." I rubbed her back and held in my grin. Her enthusiasm caught me up and swept me along with her, but we were talking about a trundier pup here, not a dog or a kitten. "I imagine things are different than, say, with Teddy."

"Teddy's yours," Missy said kindly. She lifted the pup and rubbed her chin on its head. "You have your baby, and I have mine." She leaped off my lap and darted across the bridge toward our domit.

"I could make her bring the pup back," I said, though I didn't want to be firm about this. Missy was right; the pup was in danger. Hell, I wanted to grab the little beasty and find a hiding place for her myself.

"Let her hold Laylee for now. I'll walk you back and talk with her, explain my plan. Then I'll take Laylee to a safer location."

"Okay." We walked side-by-side like parents out for an early morning stroll. I really needed to keep my mind from wandering down that lane, but it was hard. Durran was fun to be with. I liked him. It wasn't wrong to want more.

"Are you comfortable in your domit?" Durran asked.

Was he making chitchat, or did he really want to know?

"We are. It's nice of your clan to take us in and give us secure homes."

"You are welcome here. You were from the start."

"When we left Earth for Ferlaern, I never thought we'd

live in blossoms suspended from giant trees high in the canopy."

"You don't live close to nature on Earth?" He looked around with satisfaction on his face. "I can't imagine."

"We built homes out of the lumber we cut from trees."

"Why?"

I shot him a glance, unable to read his tone. His head tilted as he stared down at me, as if he were truly interested in hearing my answer.

It had been a long time since I talked with a guy I was interested in. I'd nearly blown it, spilling my guts to him about my feelings earlier. But maybe there was a spark of interest on his part. I'd watch him and see.

"Why do we cut trees and use their boards?" I asked.

He nodded.

"It's an old-fashioned way of constructing homes. Long ago, buildings were constructed of stone and mortar." I'd never thought about it. "I love how you use something that's already here for homes, rather than create something new. You live close to the land, using what nature gives you while taking care not to leave much impact on your surroundings."

"Your wood and stone homes do this as well?"

"We build out in the open, mostly, and we have huge cities with hundreds of thousands of tall buildings constructed of steel and a substance made from ground stone called concrete."

"I cannot imagine anything like that. Our villages are large but even when we combine all the clans in the low area where we spend our winters, there are only a few thousand of us."

"I like it here," I said. "It's a simple yet comforting way of life."

"I'm glad. I hope you'll always feel welcome here."

I wanted so much more than the kindness of strangers. Over the past few weeks, I watched him. He went out of his way to play with the children, even Alexa's sometimes cranky twins. When he rode his trundier, he practically melded with the creature as if they were one. Durran jumped into everything completely, something I greatly admired.

It might be wrong of me to long for someone who treated me no differently than everyone else, but I couldn't help it. It wasn't just the kind way he treated everyone or how he rode his trundier. There was something about his rich black hair shot through with purple. His horns that jutted majestically from his head. The scars networking his arms, chest, and face that told a tragic story from his past. His tail that teased my spine this very moment. Did he realize the message he sent with the caress?

Maybe not. He didn't seem aware it was happening.

When we reached my domit, Missy sat on the big rock someone left beside our door. The trundier pup snoozed on her lap while she carefully stroked its spine.

"Time to give Laylee to Durran," I said.

"Please?" Pleading came through in her voice. "Can't I keep her here?"

"She needs to be among her kind, youngling," Durran said. "Don't you agree, Rayne?" His twinkling green eyes met mine, mesmerizing me for a second. I'd never seen him even vaguely flirty.

I had to be mistaken.

"She does," I said, nodding. "She'll get stronger when she plays with the other hatchlings."

"I'll play with her," Missy said. "Please? She can sleep in my bed with me, and we'll run around with the other kids. That'll make her stronger."

"We have no idea what to feed her," I added. I was winging it here, making this up as I went along.

"Your mother's correct," Durran said, and I missed the sparkle in his eyes already. It fled as quick as it arrived. "Laylee needs to remain near the other trundiers."

"How will that keep her safe?" Missy asked, her head tilting.

Durran stooped down in front of my daughter, and his voice lowered to almost nothing. "Can you keep a secret?"

Missy nodded solemnly.

"I'm going to hide her."

My daughter's eyes lit up. "How?"

"I'll place her in a hidden nest."

"Hidden?" Missy whispered. "Like, the mean guy won't be able to find her?"

"Not if I am careful with her disguise."

"She's gonna wear a costume?" Missy asked in awe.

I loved how sweet he was with my daughter. What would it be like to share her with Durran? I was careful not to date anyone I wouldn't want as a father for my precious child. Sure, I went out with guys, but I never brought any of them home. None seemed…worthy. A snooty thought on my part, but it was true.

Durran was worthy.

"You'll be surprised what leaves can do," Durran said. "Do you think that'll be enough to keep her safe?" It was sweet of him to involve her in his plan.

"It will." Missy nodded. "Can I help make her leaf costume?"

"I have to do it in secret, but I tell you what. Come by this afternoon, and I'll not only show you how to feed her food that'll help make her strong, but we'll craft the costume together."

"Cool," Missy sighed, her eyes wide. "Can I go, Mom?"

"Of course, honey."

My heart was splitting wide open. Durran was…amazing.

"Then it's a plan."

"A plan." Missy held out her hand to shake on it, and Durran did.

He shot me a look filled with happiness, telling me he wasn't placating my daughter but involving her because he wanted to. That…wrecked me.

"You'll need to give her to me for now, though," Durran said, holding out his arms. "I'll put her in the hidden nest. Don't worry. Horesk will never find her."

Did such a place exist?

"All right," Missy said. After kissing Laylee on her ebony head, she carefully laid the creature in Durran's arms. Seeing him cradling the small, vulnerable pup made my heart melt all over again. My knees too, but there was nothing new about that. During the two weeks I lived in this village, I almost got used to feeling swoony whenever he came within twenty feet of me.

"Go inside, honey," I said, rubbing her back. "I'll be in in a few minutes."

"Okay." She dragged her feet as she turned and slipped inside.

I watched Durran to see what he'd do now. He cuddled the trundier pup and made soft coochie-coo sounds to her.

Jeez, I almost wanted to be a hatchling if he'd snuggle me and speak in my ear like he did with Laylee.

"Thank you for explaining this to Missy." I swallowed past the lump in my throat. "I hate to see her hurt. Will Laylee be safe?"

His shoulders dropped. "I'd like to say yes, but it's

going to prove a challenge. Horesk can be…relentless."

"He's the one who tried to break up Garek and Piper."

"He wishes to follow the old ways."

"We're not part of the old ways, which I imagine is a problem for Horesk."

He nodded. "I will do my best to persuade him."

Did he have any more pull that the warlord of the clan?

"I'll bring Missy later," I said. There wasn't much I could do but follow along with the plan. "Will you show both of us how we can help her? I want to be part of this, too." I stroked the creature's head and she cooed.

"Of course." He lowered the hatchling to the decking, and she remained still, staring up at him in complete adoration.

Did I look at him that way, too? Probably.

"Have you ever thought about doing karaoke?" I spontaneously asked. During our journey from Earth, my friend, Piper, talked a lot about forming a new wild west. She envisioned square dances, potluck dinners, a town with a market, and a community center where everyone could gather at the end of a long day. We all got caught up in the idea, adding our own slant to the fun things we could do. Mine was karaoke. I used to do it all the time before Missy was born. My voice wasn't anything exciting, but my enthusiasm made up for what I lacked.

He frowned.

"You don't need to know how to sing," I rushed in to say. "Really, anything works. You could hum." In my gushing, I latched onto his warm arm. It flexed beneath my fingers, and I stilled, looking down at his gorgeous scales. Sure, he had scars, but he earned them in battle against the duskhorde. They were a part of him, as much as his feet and the sparkle I savored whenever I found it in his eyes.

When I looked up, I found him closer than expected. His gaze flicked from my hand to my face then back before focusing on my mouth.

Ah… If only he'd kiss me.

"We, um…" I said. "We're holding karaoke five nights from now. At the community center."

"I see."

I could taste his lack of enthusiasm in the air. It popped my bubble.

Distraction. I needed a distraction! "And you'll speak with Horesk about giving us time to help her grow?"

"After I make sure Laylee is secure in her new nest." Steel came through in his voice as if he believed he had sway over the nasty older male.

"Let me know what he says?"

He nodded.

"Then, if you want, come back and we'll look at those samples."

"All right."

I wanted to delay this moment, drag it out for as long as possible. Once he left, I'd go inside and while my daughter and Teddy made awesome company, it wasn't the same. I was there for her and to some extent, she was there for me, but as a child, I couldn't ask for much. Same with my new kitten.

But I wasn't going to push. I'd let him lead whatever this was between us and follow. Not because I was passive but because I was afraid of scaring him away. There was something sweetly vulnerable about Durran, and I was convinced he just needed time.

I watched as he walked away, holding the tiny trundier pup close to his chest. His head bent forward as he kissed the top of her spiky head.

Rayne

Missy and I had breakfast with Piper, her son Noah, and her maelstrom mate, Garek.

The Ferlaern mated, which was pretty much like a marriage back on Earth, but on rare occasions a couple would form a maelstrom mating. From what I could tell, it meant the couple were soulmates. From the moment they met, they'd be filled with an overwhelming desire to be together. And once their bond solidified, matching symbols would appear on their right shoulders.

I'd seen Piper's and had to admit I felt envy.

The kids teased each other and Piper and Garek could barely take their eyes and hands off each other. I moped, wishing Durran was here, flirting with me.

Outside the dining hall, we stopped to visit further.

Piper leaned back against Garek. His big hands cupped her shoulders like she was a delicate glass sculpture, and she leaned her head against his arm then kissed his wrist.

My heart ached. I wanted something like that. I wanted it with Durran.

Stepping forward, Piper stooped down in front of

Missy. "Garek, Noah, and I are going to the hatchling grounds to work with Noah's trundier," she said, her gaze shooting to me for advance permission. When I nodded, she continued. "Do you want to come? It's the perfect chance to learn some of the early things you need to do to deepen the bond with a hatchling. Someday, maybe you'll form your own bond, and then you'll be ahead."

Before we left for breakfast, I cautioned Missy not to mention Laylee. Until we were sure she was safe, it would be best to keep her secret.

Missy leaped around. "Yes. Yes! I wanna go." She grabbed my hand and tugged on it. "Can I, Mom? Can I?"

"Of course." I stroked her hair. I wasn't thrilled at the thought of my daughter riding a giant hornet, but it was clear the creature wouldn't grow overnight. And it was equally clear Missy's heart was locked on the trundiers. I'd be mean to keep her away.

I had time to adjust while Missy had time to learn and grow. Hopefully, she wouldn't ride one alone until she was sixteen. Or thirty.

"Then let's go." Piper held her hand out to Missy and gave me a soft smile. "I know you have research to do. Go ahead, and we'll bring her back by lunchtime."

"Thanks."

I returned to my domit and got things ready.

In a short time, someone scratched on the door—a Ferlaern thing. I opened the membrane to find Durran waiting. My heart skipped a beat, and it was all I could do not to swoon. What would he do if I did something like that?

Instead, I waved for him to enter. "Perfect timing. I was about to get my microscope out."

I tucked the door closed, shutting us both inside.

"Have a seat on the sofa, if you'd like," I said, then sucked in a breath as memories of me grinding against him flooded my mind. Flames to my cheeks followed, my overheated blood surging through my veins like liquid fire. "Or maybe not." No need to take him to the scene of our most recent crime.

He remained in the tiny entry, looking poised to fidget. "I have something for you."

"Oh!" This was exciting.

I smiled as he handed me a bright red, dead beetle about the size of a computer mouse.

"Thanks," I said. Crap. What was I supposed to do with it?

As if he heard my thoughts, he took it from me with a flash of his tusks that made my knees turn to pudding. Really, if he nudged me, I'd topple over. Hopefully onto a bed with him following me down to the surface.

Earth—no, Ferlaern—to Rayne. Pay attention.

"I cleaned it," he said, tapping the back of the insect.

"Good. I wouldn't want to hold a dirty beetle."

"I meant the innards. I cleaned them out."

"Even better," I said brightly.

He turned it over and revealed four long legs and a smooth, black belly. "Presenting this to you is part of Ferlaern tradition."

Like bringing casseroles to a new neighbor. "Giving someone a beetle is a tradition?"

"Yes. I would also like to take you hunting."

"For liscards?"

His eyes gleamed, though I wasn't sure what was funny about my question. "No, something smaller. We could share the kill."

I wasn't opposed to hunting. After all, I enjoyed eating meat. But I wasn't sure I was eager to shoot a doe-like creature in the forest. But this was a chance to spend time with Durran. I wouldn't pass that up, though I wasn't sure about a sorta date that involved death. "I'd like that," I said with forced cheer. "Whenever you want to go hunting, let me know and I'll arrange for someone to watch Missy."

He flashed his tusks again, and I swore relief smoothed the lines on his face. "Good. Good." Lifting the beetle, he carefully attached it to my hair like a big, red, fancy clip. So… this was kinda cute. It was a gift. A dead beetle gift, but I'd treasure it always because Durran gave it to me.

"Thank you." I smiled up at him. "How does it look?"

"You're gorgeous," he said in a husky voice that channeled right through me. If he kept at it, my panties were going to be soaked.

I whirled around, and the skirt of my dress flared out. "Let's sit at the table, shall we? As you can see, I set up the microscope already." In my excitement, I did it last night. "We can take a look at those samples. I prepped everything already." Smoothing my skirt, I took one of the seats and patted the other.

Durran settled on the wooden surface and studied the microscope.

"My precious baby," I said, stroking the white-painted metal arm. "I bought it with babysitting money in high school and have hung onto it since. I used to love finding bugs and odd vegetation and looking at them under the light. My dad rigged this one to function with solar power and it's freshly charged up."

I turned it on and focused on the first slide then slid the device closer to Durran, who watched me more than our science project. "This slide shows a scraping from beneath the bark of a healthy tree. I went to the edge of the forest the other day to find appropriate samples of trees that don't appear impacted by whatever's harming the ones supporting our domits."

"You went to the edge of the forest alone?" he basically shouted.

"Um, yeah." I nudged the microscope closer and tapped the top.

At my direction, he peered through the lens. "Oh. Amazing."

"And if you'll let me…" I slid the second slide onto the stage. "Can you see the difference? I'm not sure what this substance is but it's not an insect or any spore I've seen before."

"It does look different," he said. "What do you suspect it is?"

I shrugged. "I only have a theory."

"What is it?"

"Since I found the same substance in the soil beneath the tree, my guess is that the tree is pulling it up along with water it takes from the soil."

"It's something in the ground around it."

"Yup."

"Something natural or something placed there by…"

I huffed out a breath, sending my bangs shooting upward. "Exactly. I hope this is natural, that it's a process the trees go through, and we can somehow mediate the effect until it passes, but if…"

"If it's someone purposefully poisoning the trees," he finished for me.

"Then we have to catch and stop them."

"We need to do more investigation around the trees. We can look for tracks and the clan can set guards. I'll speak with Garek."

"That's a great idea. We can also go farther afield to see if other trees are impacted."

His probing gaze met mine, and despite the serious subject, my spine tingled. But then, I was sitting close to Durran. Pretty much a dream come true.

"Why don't we do this when we go hunting?" he suggested.

"Sure." I grinned, liking the idea of spending time with him. "How about tomorrow after breakfast? The sooner we get to the bottom of this, the better."

He nodded and shyly flashed his tusks. His gaze went to the beetle that surprisingly hadn't fallen off my head. Perhaps the long legs held it in place.

Durran smelled good, like sunshine and male. I wanted to lean forward, close my eyes, and breathe him in.

His gaze dropped to my lips. Was he remembering our kiss? Hell, was he remembering what happened on my sofa?

I was. I wanted that again. No, I wanted more.

Heat pooled low in my belly, and my panties went wet.

As if he could tell, his pupils widened, making more warmth flood my limbs. We were supposed to be working with the samples, maybe coming up with more theories, but all I could think of was his cock. I hadn't seen it, and I wanted to touch it. Lick it.

He stood and shoved his chair back then pushed the table away. My precious microscope rocked but he righted it. He turned and dropped to his knees in front of me.

"I'm grateful you're wearing my crustian," he said.

It was all I could do to speak. Why was he kneeling in front of me?

"Is a crustian the beetle?" Was that my voice all husky and full of need?

His hands landed on my thighs, the warmth of them flooding through the thin material of my dress.

"Rayne," he said, looking up as if asking permission.

Do it, I wanted to shout. Do whatever they hell you want with my body.

"Durran?" My throat was half closed off, and my body strung tighter than a spring.

"May I?" he asked, his fingers teasing the hem of my skirt.

"Yes," I whispered.

One corner of his lips curled up. So damn sexy.

He reached behind my waist and slid my body forward on the chair until I crested the edge. Then, while watching my face, he slowly slid my dress up to my waist, revealing my panties. I was overheated down there. How could I be anything else?

This was crazy. What were we doing?

He eased off my panties, tossing them aside, and nudged my legs apart.

Fuck, fuck.

Who the hell cared what we were doing? I was here for the ride.

Ride. Pretty please.

He stroked down my slit with his thumb then leaned forward. Parting my saturated lips, he exposed me to him and exhaled on my clit.

My eyes rolled back in my head. I jerked forward until I was almost laying on the chair, my legs splayed wide, and my cunt lying open to him to do whatever he pleased.

He hitched my legs up onto his shoulders then shot me a grin. "You smell amazing."

I smelled like an aroused woman, a common occurrence around Durran.

This was…unbelievable. I never dreamed we'd do this in the middle of my science experiment.

His fingers teased through my wet folds. I was slick. Wanting.

With a groan, he dropped his head and placed his mouth on my clit. His tongue stroked it while his finger slid inside me.

Crap. I tipped my head back on the chair and moaned.

"Yes," he said. "Tell me what you feel."

"Fuck, Durran, it's amazing. Don't stop."

"Don't stop this?" His fingers stilled inside me.

"You're a fuckin' tease."

"It's only a tease if I don't give you complete satisfaction. And I will. Never fear." His mouth returned to my flesh, and he licked and sucked while his fingers pumped deeply inside me.

My muscles tensed. My body arched on the chair, straining to take everything he had to give.

His fingers went faster. I bucked and strained forward, eager to feel it all.

When he gently rolled my clit between his tusks, I shrieked.

My keen shot through the domit as I crashed into a billion pieces in his mouth.

He stroked my folds as I came down from the best orgasm of my life. With the way he kept topping the last, I could only look forward to the next.

Carefully, he licked me clean, gently sucking up every drop of my satisfaction. Then he tucked my dress back down around my legs and eased me back on the chair with a half-smile on his face.

He retook the seat beside me, but he didn't look my way. "So, tell me what other theories you have about our trees."

11

Durran

Rayne and I discussed a few more theories about the trees, but we came to no conclusions. She walked with me outside, and we stood on the walkway pretending nothing happened inside her domit.

"I'll see you later in the hatchling grounds?" I asked, maintaining the ruse.

She fed me a half-smile, but I didn't miss the shadows lurking in her eyes. "Missy and I will be there."

The walkway shuddered, and we both grabbed the rail. Our attention flew to the canopy above, and I groaned when I saw how pale the leaves were. Hunks of bark flaked off the tree and rained down on us, clattering on the wooden decking.

"They're dying," Rayne said, tears in her eyes.

"How much time do you think we have?"

"Not enough. I need to test those samples. I brought solutions with me that can check for chemicals." She shrugged. "I wasn't sure when I'd ever need them, but I hated to leave them behind. I thought... Well, I thought thcy might come in handy if I wanted to run some general tests. Nothing as horrifying as this."

"Why don't you do that, and I'll look for Garek? He needs to know what's going on."

She nodded. "He went to the hatchling grounds with Piper, Noah, and Missy. When we meet up later, I hope I have answers."

I left, making plans for what I'd feed Laylee. So many worries. Our trees dying—where would we live if we no longer had our domits? The low birthrate of trundier pups. Rayne was right; each should be treasured no matter its size. Dolcing for any reason needed to be a thing of the past.

After checking on Laylee and finding her sleeping, hidden under a pile of leaves in the abandoned nest, I located Garek sitting with Piper on a bench near the nest with Noah's trundier pup.

Joining them on the bench, I explained the situation with our trees.

"This is horrible," Piper exclaimed, her wide-eyed gaze meeting Garek's. "We have to do something."

"Rayne is running samples and when she knows the cause, we can treat it." I hoped there was a treatment. "She believes someone is poisoning the trees."

"Why?" Piper asked before her face fell. "Oh. Do you think someone's trying to drive us from the valley? My first guess is the duskhorde. They can't reach us up here and they want mates." She shuddered, likely remembering when they attacked.

"Or they hope to drive the trundiers to the ground," I said grimly. "They enjoy eating the hatchlings."

Piper squeezed Garek's hand. "We need to save the forest."

"You're right," Garek said, standing. "I'll post guards to

watch the trees, but I need to speak with Narcial about this." He bent forward and kissed Piper. "I'll see you later at our domit?"

"Yup." Her arms went around his shoulders, and he scooped her up to further their kiss. Envy filled me. Would Rayne and I ever develop a relationship like this? I gave her pleasure, but I didn't know what the incident meant.

She hadn't been humoring me, had she?

Fuck. I needed to stop thinking like this. I shook off the thought the moment it hit me. No one had an orgasm to humor someone else. But I still wasn't sure how what happened between us should be interpreted.

Asking was an option.

Except... Asking could lead to rejection, just as it had when I was young. I couldn't take that chance. Patience was the best way to handle this. I would court her. Then and only then, I would ask her to be my mate. By then, I'd know what this all meant.

As Garek left, Piper nodded goodbye and climbed up into the nest to join Noah and Missy.

I left the hatchling grounds with one goal in mind. Finding Horesk. It was time to tell him how this was going to be. We would be given a chance to strengthen Laylee. He could hold off his dolcing decision for a moon or more.

But when he wasn't at his domit. I went to the dining area but couldn't locate him there. Striding to the high council chamber, I scratched on the door.

"Enter," someone called from inside, and I lifted the flap and entered the large domit.

Elder Enok sat on a cushion on the floor, with a pot of tea in front of him.

"Yes?" Enok asked, his head tilting. Pale lavender streaked through his graying hair, and fine wrinkles covered his face. "Do you have need of an elder, Durran?"

"Do you know where I can find Horesk?" I asked after giving him a low bow. "I'm looking for him specifically."

"He went to the Nulet Clan."

The clan was run by my friend, Bruge. "Do you know when Horesk will return?"

"A few sunslices? I am not sure, however. Would you like me to send a message to him?"

"No, that won't be necessary." My gut eased. If he was gone for sunslices, we had a small reprieve with Laylee.

"Very well, then." Enok lifted his tea and took a long swallow. "Is there anything else I can help you with?"

"No." I backed toward the door. "Thank you."

"You're welcome, Durran."

My next stop was Narcial's domit. Once Garek was finished speaking with her, I needed to ask her advice.

All the way across the village, I thought about Rayne.

Yesterday, she rubbed herself against me on her sofa. Watching her face while she found bliss with me—me! — couldn't be topped.

But then…

Fuck, I licked her. Sucked on her clit. Pushed my fingers inside her until she came in the sweetest way imaginable. If she were nearby and receptive, I'd drop to my knees and do it all over again.

What did it mean? Did she like me or…? I wasn't sure what else I could believe.

How could any female as wonderful as Rayne want a male like me? I was quiet, surly much of the time, and scarred. She could do much better.

I didn't know what to think of all this, but one thing was clear. She tasted amazing. My cock twitched, eager to be buried inside her, and the culier strands elongated. My cock would need to wait—maybe forever.

Deciding to give Garek and Narcial time to talk, I went

to my domit, where I grabbed my small bow and a fletch of arrows.

I left our village on the northern side. A slunkette pack foraged in the forest higher up the mountain. It wouldn't take long to track them down, select the weakest to shoot, clean it, then store it in leaf packets near the trundiers. Later, when Missy and Rayne arrived to help me with Laylee, I could show them the other hatchlings after we fed and exercised Laylee. I was proud of how strong and healthy they were. I took good care of our trundiers. This was another way to win a mate, by showing her I was a contributing member of our Clan.

When I reached the forest floor, I headed down a trail, picking up my pace to a ground-eating jog. I left the bustle of the village behind and continued through the densest part of the jungle, running until my heart pounded in my chest and my breathing was ragged. It felt good to be here, as if the forest and I were one.

It rained at this elevation this morning, and the air hung thick with moisture. A few brave flesers buzzed close, hoping for a bite, but I brushed them away.

I slowed to a walk, and took my time, studying the enormous trees, the ferns towering over me, and the few ground-nesting birds poking their heads through the lush vegetation along the narrow path. In a small clearing to my right, a male endla extended his plumes and strutted around a female with his wings extended. The endla mating dance. If I danced for Rayne, would she smile?

The trees appeared healthy in this part of the forest, which was interesting. I'd tell Rayne when she came to the hatchling grounds.

I kept my footsteps silent. Good thing. If I'd been loud, they would've heard me.

A soft rustling ahead made me pause. The noise felt off,

as if it wasn't part of the forest. It wasn't a liscard or the slunkette pack I sought.

It belonged to beings like me.

My heart stalled, and my throat went dry.

Were other Ferlaern traveling to my village?

Remaining on the path wasn't an option, not until I knew what I was dealing with. I leaped up and grabbed a branch then swung my foot up, hooking it. As the sounds came closer, my pulse bounded in my throat. I stood on the branch and went higher, snaking around the trunk until the canopy disguised me from whatever would pass below.

Lying on a wide branch, I peered down at the trail. Would they use it or find a different way to move through the forest?

Footsteps drew closer, and they were doing an excellent job of masking themselves. If I hadn't paused to watch the endla's mating dance, I might've walked right up on them.

I sensed four or five moving closer. A scouting party?

I suppressed my growl when five of the duskhorde strode beneath me.

They wore no clothing, and their sizeable cocks swung between their legs. One paused and lifted his hand, stilling the others.

I stopped breathing.

His big, knobby head jutting from his hunched shoulders twisted and turned as he studied the area.

Hunched low, I tried to blend with the branch, but they didn't look up. My heart thudded faster than a galloping liscard as I watched.

Dark fur draped down their torsos, and a single horn speared from their heads. They used it to impale their victims; my chest bore a scar that matched the width of a dusklen horn. Only by diving to the side had I avoided death.

The lead dusklen's beady red eyes flicked right and left, and his claws clenched to fist.

My mind was dragged back to claws like these raking my face, shoulders, and chest before I fought the creature off. I'd killed him but my body had been left in tatters.

The dusklen's hand dropped, and the pack continued moving nearly silent through the forest, heading in a direction that would take them near my village.

They knew we lived—and protected—this area. To come here after we drove them away a few cycles ago was not only bold on their part, but it was also disturbing. This showed intent. Why were they here? It was rare to see the duskhorde beyond the low plain where we spent our winters.

Only two things would draw them to the forest.

The unhatched trundiers and the Earthling women.

They continued down the trail, and I climbed down to the ground and took off after them, shadowing them as they drew close to the village. They peered up into the canopy, speaking with each other in a hand gesture language I didn't understand.

I followed them as they skirted the trundier landing platform and jogged up the pass, leaving our valley.

Then I returned to the canopy and sought out Garek, filling him in on my latest discovery.

"All of this spells trouble," he said, pacing the small open area in his ruling domit. His tail whipped up as he thudded his fist on the smooth surface of his ulan wood desk. The prentise bug lamp sitting on one side rocked. "We can't guard everything all the time. There aren't enough of us."

"When we join up with the other clans in the lowlands, we can share the duty, though that won't protect the trees in the valleys."

"We won't meet up for a few more moons. And that raises the question. Should we leave warriors here to guard the trees? We can't risk them while we're gone."

"Splitting us up is never a good idea. I understand why we do it during the summer months. The resources in each valley are limited. It makes sense to divide us into four groups." I ran agitated fingers through my hair. "I love how we live solely with our clans for the summer moons but…"

His perceptive gaze met mine. "You think we should combine clans here as well."

"It isn't the best option, but protection needs to be our priority." My grumble rang out in the small domit. "We'll be crowded but we'll have more warriors to protect our precious females from the duskhorde and watch the trees."

"This assumes whatever's happening to the trees here is also happening in the other valleys. I'll send zisk birds to the other clans and ask. We can talk about options once we know what we're dealing with. If it's just here…"

"It points to this being a person's actions rather than something cyclical."

"Yes." His lips thinned. "And as for the duskhorde… I don't wish to start a war, but we cannot let them come here whenever they please. I tried to form a treaty, but you know what happened with that."

They sent a severed Ferlaern head as their answer.

"We don't have many options." Garek gnashed his tusks. "We'll convene the warlords when we're together in the lowlands this winter and discuss how to proceed from there. Until then, I'll double the guards on the trees and the village perimeter."

"Let me know when I can take a shift."

I left him with unease churning through me.

I didn't like this, not one bit.

12

Durran

The best way to distract myself from my worry about the duskhorde and our trees would be to focus on courting Rayne. As much as I wanted to solve our problems, we had a plan in place.

Arriving at Narcial's home, I scratched on her door, and she called out, encouraging me to enter.

Her solemn gaze met mine. "This news about our trees is devastating. That and the duskhorde, but Garek and I agreed he'd share the news first with an official elder council and then with our warriors."

I nodded slowly. "I have faith Rayne will be able to reverse the damage to the trees. She says they could recover as long as the cause is discovered and stopped."

"We are fortunate to have her living in our clan." Very. "I will speak with her as I was long ago taught which herbs could strengthen our trees. She and I can make a brew and pour it on the roots."

"Let me know when you go to the ground, and I will go with you."

She dipped her head forward. "Very well." Her sigh

bled from her frail lungs. "I imagine you did not come here to speak to me about the trees, however."

"Do you have a munette to talk, wise one?" I said, bowing low to show my infinite respect for this elder.

"Of course, Durran." She waved to her sofa. "Sit. Would you like tea?"

"No, thank you."

"Ah," she said, studying my face. "This is also serious, then?"

"Yes."

Her breath caught, and she dropped down opposite me, in a chair. "Tell me your thoughts, then. Let me see if I can help."

I got right to it. "How does one properly court a female?"

Her thick brow ridge lifted, and while her posture didn't loosen, her lips quirked up briefly. "You know our traditions. Follow them and your courtship will be well received."

"What if this female is not of our species?"

"You speak of an Earthling." Her crotchety voice lifted. "Any female in particular?"

"Rayne." I breathed the name. Her voice. Her scent. Her sweet ways. Winning her affection was my sole wish.

"Ah, yes." She flashed her tusks and eased back on the chair cushions. "You are smart to choose this particular female."

I swore her eyes sparkled with glee, but I must be mistaken. "She is lovely."

"I see more than just her appearance, and I imagine you do as well. This one has a big heart." The skin around her eyes wrinkled. "Almost as big as yours, my friend."

A big heart, eh? "It is not always wise to care." I thought of Horesk and the churning feelings I carried for him since I was a small youngling and discovered his role —or lack of role—in my life. "I protect my heart." My feet shifted on the membranous floor in agitation.

I tried to tell myself I didn't care about Horesk. He tossed me aside and was no longer worthy of even a scratch along the surface of my heart.

He rejected me.

"You think your heart is secure?" she asked with one lifted brow. "That you can secure it from everyone? I say no. You don't give yourself easily, but when you do, it is complete," she said with a pert nod.

Had I given my heart to Rayne already? Perhaps. She was all I could think of. Dream of. So many wishes wrapped up in one precious female.

"Perhaps," was all I was willing to say.

"However, you are here for advice, so I will give it," she said. "It is unknown how Earthling females will respond to a traditional Ferlaern courtship, but it is good to test them out while incorporating a few Earthling customs as well." She bared her aged tusks and tapped her bony chest. "It is good you came to me. I have studied the Earthlings, and I believe I have learned their ways."

I leaned forward, eager to hear all she could tell me. "What is the best way to win an Earthling female?"

"There are likely many ways, but I have heard they enjoy flowers."

I blinked slowly, trying to remember if Rayne paid any attention to vegetation outside the trees. Oh, yes, she said she did scapes of the land and that she enjoyed foliage. "Flowers in particular? Shrubs will not work as well?"

"Flowers. You know, blossoms."

"We live in blossoms." I frowned, uncertain about this. "How can I do something for Rayne that involves our domits? She lives in one already so gifting her with a new one makes no sense. They are all the same, and she will not need another until for another cycle."

"You ask for advice, and I give it freely." She huffed. "What you do with my suggestions is for you to decide, of course. I can only impart what I have learned. Believe me, I have studied this. I even questioned a few females as I was intrigued to understand their differences. How else can I meld our traditions together to move forward as one?"

"I appreciate that you do this."

She shrugged. "If we don't include them, any young they bear will feel torn between our two worlds. I do not wish this for our future."

Narcial was the wise one here, not me.

One of her brow ridges lifted. "But if flowers are all you wish to hear about then we are—"

"No!" I swallowed and continued in a normal tone. "I am happy to listen to whatever you have to offer, naturally," I hurried to say, eager to assure her I appreciated her comments.

But…flowers? My spine stiffened. I would find a way.

"I heard they enjoy candy, though I am not sure what that is," Narcial continued, ticking each item off on her spindly fingers. "You will have to ask one of the others. Perhaps it can be foraged from the forest floor. Piper may be able to tell you what it is."

"I thought of asking her advice."

Her brow narrowed. "You went to her first?"

"No, no." I scrambled to find a way to avoid giving offense. "Piper may know Rayne well, but I knew you would have the best suggestions."

"See? You are wise after all."

Leaning forward, I waited on her every word.

"I hear them speak all the time about pockets and their

need for more, though I am not sure what this means, so I suggest you don't try to gift Rayne empty pockets."

I bowed my head, soaking this in. "Anything else?"

"Jewelry."

"I gave her a crustian."

"Cleaned, I hope."

"Of course! I would not give it to her in any other way."

Flapping her feet to show her excitement, she grunted. "Very good. See? I said you were smart."

Smart, perhaps, but I didn't know how to truly court her. And we did…things that weren't part of a regular courtship.

Should I tell Narcial I kissed Rayne, that we rubbed together on her sofa, and that I sucked her clit until she came?

Probably not.

"There are other things I have heard Earthlings enjoy," Narcial said sagely. She leaned back on the cushions. "They enjoy pedis."

"What is a pedi?" I would try to find one if I could.

"It is my understanding that the female sits in a chair while someone pampers her feet and does something odd to her nails." Shaking her finger at me, her face went completely serious. "You need to know, however, that Earthling females do not have claws on their toes. Do not be offended, no matter what, if you see them! If you mock their feet or suggest they are unworthy without claws, they will not like this."

"That is good to know." Would I mock Rayne for not having claws? I doubted this. If anyone understood how unimportant one's physical appearance was, it was me.

"They do have short nails," she scoffed, "but they are nothing like the lovely claws our females possess."

I nodded, sucking in her every word. Frankly, I didn't mind a female with no claws. We rarely fought with our feet anymore and if needed, I could protect Rayne from any danger. She would not need to battle.

"One other thing that might help win her heart," Narcial said slyly.

Why act like this is a big secret?

Wait. Maybe it was. This could be the final, most important key to unlocking an Earthling's heart. "What is it?"

"Karaoke."

My brows drew together. "I am happy to try anything, but what is this?" Rayne mentioned it earlier. It was—

"Singing."

I reeled backward, my spine shoving against the back of the sofa. "I cannot sing."

"Not even to win Rayne's heart?"

How horrifying. But, if it would please Rayne, I would do it. "What kind of singing must I do?"

"They are hosting an event in the…carmunity center, I believe this is what they call the large domit near the dining area?"

"Community center, yes."

"Yes, that's it. I have heard Rayne loves to sing and during karaoke, she willingly sings with others, doing this karaoke. You do not wish her to sing with other males, I imagine."

"Truly, no."

"See?" She tapped her temple. "Smart. They are holding an event in five sunslices, after the sun has left our glorious sky. At the carmunity center."

"I will be there," I vowed, my fist to my chest. But sing…? I wasn't sure about this.

"Very good, then." Rising, she strode to the door but

turned back to glance my way. "Will you remain on my sofa all day?"

"What? No. Sorry." I rose and followed her outside.

She stopped at her long row of pots and knelt in front of them. She didn't look up, just pulled tiny weeds from the soil and tossed them over the walkway to the ground. "You will go to this singing of the karaoke and join Rayne when she screeches?"

"I doubt she screeches."

"Have you heard them sing yet?"

"I have not." My feet shuffled on the wooden decking. "But I will not grimace, no matter what it sounds like."

"Very good."

"I don't know, though," I said. I tried to avoid social gatherings where others stared.

"I know just the song you need to sing with Rayne."

Naturally, she did.

My spine cringed and my tail whipped back and forth behind me, but I braced myself. "You know I'm not eager to do this."

"I give you the tip to please one particular Earthling, and you throw it away." She turned her perceptive gaze toward me. Settling back on her heels, she flashed her tusks. "Don't you wish to make Rayne smile? Others will if you do not."

"Many would like to mate with her."

"But who would *she* like to mate with?" She flicked out her hand. "You're a brave warrior and the head trainer of our trundier. Even more, you're heir to your uncle's powldron once he hands it to you."

"My uncle is young. Healthy." May he hold onto his powldron for many cycles. While I looked forward to a warlord role, I was in no rush to lead. I liked my simple life here, tending the trundiers.

"This is not the point," she said reasonably. "Do you deny you have much to offer a female?"

"You know it's about more than my status in the Willen Clan or my ability to train trundiers."

Her tusks flashed again. "It is. It is about the heart. The second heart, to be specific."

"You speak of a maelstrom bond." I'd be foolish to dream of something like that with Rayne. "Even if mine beat for her, I doubt hers will match with mine."

"You really won't know unless you try, now will you?"

"She could have anyone." I stated it plainly.

"She could also have you." Narcial rose slowly to her feet and stretched her spine and tail. "My bones don't like me gardening any longer, but I ignore them."

"I see." I had work to do. Hunting for Laylee, and I needed to prepare myself for Missy and Rayne joining me in the nesting grounds this afternoon. Our trees… I wanted to wing to the next valley where the Willen Clan lived to see if their trees were affected. I needed to figure out how to incorporate some Earth traditions into my courtship.

I was beginning to doubt everything that happened with Rayne. The rubbing on her sofa, the kiss, and even me licking her clit until she shuddered in my mouth. They were aberrations. She hadn't meant for anything like that to happen. She'd slipped, and her lips somehow ended up on mine. I slipped and my lips accidentally ended up on her clit.

Well, I needed to be honest. No true accident there. But given a choice, would she want something like that to happen again?

"How do you know what she wants unless you ask her?" Narcial asked. "Durran." She stroked my face like my mother used to when I was young. Before she died and my father rejected me. "Rayne *sees* you."

Did I dare join her for this event in a public place? I grumbled. "What is the song?"

"I will write down the words for you and put them in your domit. Study them. Memorize them. Be ready to ask her to join you in this song." She turned back to her garden. "I don't know the name, but this song is sung between lions."

"What is a lion?"

"A creature living in Earth's jungle."

I frowned. "And they sing to each other?" Would I be expected to howl like a beast?

"These beasts sing in the visual adaptation Missy told me about," Narcial said. "One of Rayne's favorites."

"You mean a movie? Rayne mentioned them to me." She also offered to show me what she meant. I would ask about it later. Perhaps it would help me better understand the song I must sing. However, if this beast song were Rayne's favorite, I would read the words over and over until I knew them by heart. "Thank you, Narcial," I said, turning to leave.

She dropped back down to her knees to work on her garden, yanking out a larger weed and flinging it up over the railing. "Oh, youngling?" she called out.

I paused on the walk. "Yes?" I'd retrieve my weapons and track down a plump slunkette for Laylee's dinner.

"Remember what I said," Narcial said. "Rayne already sees you."

I wasn't sure I wanted her to fully see me. It was hard feeling vulnerable, as if my chest were pried open and my heart—my two hearts—were laid bare for her to see.

I didn't worry she'd crush them.

I worried she wouldn't even notice I was exposed.

13

Rayne

"It's some sort of chemical," I hissed, staring down at the results of my tests. "Unless it's growing here naturally, someone is dumping something toxic onto the soil beneath the trees and it's killing them."

Knowing the cause should make me feel better, but how could it? Someone wanted to destroy our way of life, and we had to stop them.

Tomorrow, when we went hunting, I could show Durran the exact substance causing harm, assuming I could locate it beneath the trees. In my soil samples, I picked up a few mangled leaves. When I studied them and did a comparison to the toxin harming the trees, it was clear that when crushed, the leaves released the toxin. It was leaching up into the trees and tainting the wood beneath the bark, slowly killing the plant.

Sitting back in my chair, I stroked my microscope, grateful I brought it with me. Otherwise, would we have discovered the cause? I needed to run a few more tests; I'd do that this evening. If we carefully removed the soil around the roots and replaced it with untainted dirt, we might be able to save the trees.

I couldn't wait to tell Durran.

Standing, I groaned as I stretched my aching spine. I was bent over my microscope for so long, my back froze in that position.

"Ten minutes, Missy. Then we're leaving," I called up the stairwell. She was playing with Teddy, and it adored her so much, I was afraid I lost my bedmate already.

Perhaps when Durran came back later to help me with my experiments, we'd fall into another spontaneous sexual encounter.

One of these days, we needed to talk about what we were doing and where it was heading, if anywhere. For now, I'd stick to my vow to remain patient. When he was ready, he'd share his thoughts.

In between then, I'd share his body…

I needed to get ready to leave for the trundier hatchling grounds. My heart pattered at the thought of seeing Durran again.

It was silly to worry about what I was going to wear. I was doing this to help my daughter—and Durran—care for the baby trundier. For all I knew, we'd muck out the nest. Did they muck out nests? The hatchlings must poop. Someone had to clean it up. Even if the parents did the dirty work, there was no momma trundier watching over Laylee.

I tugged on a pair of jeans and contorted myself to see how they must make my ass look. Being fresh out of mirrors wasn't always a bad thing.

Okay, so if Durran happened to be behind me and he happened to look down and happened to study my ass, I was rocking these jeans. They weren't mom jeans; these were magical. They had an inner panel that tucked things in where you'd rather not jiggle. They molded my thighs in a good way.

For a top, I went casual with one of my t-shirts with *Earthlings Do it Better* emblazoned in sparkling letters on the front.

Would he take me up on my offer of karaoke night at the ye olde community domit? We built a small stage. There was no mic, but most of us could raise our voice enough to be heard. And we'd talked fluff ball creatures the Ferlaern called a band into practicing tunes to play for background music.

"You ready, honey?" I called out to Missy again. "It's time to leave."

"Almost!"

Someone scratched on the door, and I walked over and lifted the flap to the side.

"Oh, hi, Crall," I said, wishing I pretended I wasn't home.

"These are for you," he said, holding out a cluster of branches topped with leaves.

"Um, thank you." What was I supposed to do with them? When Durran gave the beetle hair clip to me, it reminded me I knew next to nothing about Ferlaern traditions. The beetle felt right, if unusual. Branches? Not so much. But then, neither did Crall.

He shouldered his way inside. "I am grateful you have accepted my courtship overture."

"If you mean taking the branches from you, then here." I thrust them against his chest, releasing them whether he choose to take them or not. They clattered on the floor.

Staring down, he frowned. "That wasn't nice."

"Maybe I'm not in a nice mood." I backed away from

him until my butt hit my table. My microscope rocked, and I grabbed it before it fell over.

Crall came up behind me fast, pressing himself against my back.

Yuck, he had a hard on.

A mix of fear and irritation sparked inside me. He wouldn't push this, would he? Actually, he already was, coming here with his branches to give with conditions then acting upset when I wasn't grateful to receive them.

"Back away," I said firmly, turning to press my hand against his chest.

"You owe me. When a courtship gift is accepted, it comes with a price."

"That's not true."

His head dove down, but I squirmed, and his lips hit my chin instead of my mouth.

"Let me go," I shrieked.

"A kiss for my offering," he mumbled against my neck.

"No kiss. I refused your offering." I kicked and smacked his chest.

He backed away, his hands lifting. "This… This… I am a mighty warrior."

"So are all the Ferlaern."

His snarl ripped through the room. "You think you are special, but you are one of many Earthling females."

"We're all special." Really? Where did he get the nerve?

"You're going to regret turning down my suit."

This, I doubted. "I told you no already, and I meant it." Straightening my clothing, I prayed my shaking hands weren't apparent. He came across as someone who sought vulnerability then took advantage. "Leave. Don't come back again."

His gaze flicked to my hair. "Who gave you that?"

I blinked. "What?"

"The crustian you wear in your hair."

My chin lifted. "Durran gave it to me."

"You turn me down but seem happy to wear another male's gift."

"That should tell you I'm not interested in you."

"I want a mate," he growled. "You're a female who came here to mate with a Ferlaern."

I pointed to the door. "If you don't go, I'll scream. And I'll go directly to Garek and complain about your behavior."

"You will not." Hands lifted, he stormed toward me.

Teddy leaped down the stairs and launched herself off the back of the sofa. She landed on the back of Crall's neck, her claws digging deeply.

He whirled around, bellowing, and I plucked Teddy from his shoulder before he smacked her. I stomped to the door and lifted the flap. "Go. I mean it. Don't come back here again."

Without another word, he fled my domit.

I stepped outside and watched until he reached the next platform and kept going. Only then did my heart rate return to a more normal pace. Back inside, I collapsed on the sofa and dropped Teddy onto my lap. Leaning over, I kissed the top of her head.

"You're the best watch kitty ever. Thank you."

She purred and nuzzled my hand.

I told myself Crall got the message. He wouldn't come here again. To be on the safe side, I'd mention this to Garek. I didn't need his intervention, but he needed to know how one of the males treated me.

Footsteps padded overhead and I was grateful Missy missed Crall's "visit".

As she came down the stairs, I shoved the incident with Crall from my mind.

"Oh," I said when she joined me in the living room. Maybe I should've been more concerned about what *she* was wearing. "That's not the best outfit to wear while caring for a wild creature."

"Laylee isn't wild." Missy skipped across the room looking ready for a royal engagement. Or a ball. "I'm a princess, right?" She stuck her lower lip out in a well-practiced pout. "Princesses wear dresses."

"Princesses also wear jeans." It was a struggle, but I withheld my eye roll. About six months before leaving Earth, Missy declared herself a princess and insisted she needed to wear royal gowns. Like the devoted mom I was (sometimes), I hit thrift shops and bought a variety of flower girl dresses. Impractical, but cheap. Missy wore them to school, to the park, and I threw them into the wash, trimming off any random bit of lace that came loose and dangled after they'd finished in the dryer. "Go change."

"Please, Mommy? I want to be pretty for the trundiers."

"You'll be on your knees, playing with Laylee," I said, striving to sound reasonable. My daughter got her stubbornness from me and damn, she wore it proudly.

"I won't get dirty. Promise."

Thankfully, it wasn't hard to do laundry here. A particular creature lived in this part of the forest, digging with its snout for roots and bugs. It went to the river after eating to fill a sack on its back with water. The Ferlaern discovered if they snuck up while the creature was pouring water into the pouch with its snout, they could toss their clothing inside. The pouch sealed and the creature waddled back into the forest. When the Ferlaern dangled what vaguely looked like an enormous cat toy in front of the creature, it gave chase. The pouch sloshed, the clothing was cleaned, and when the creature was worn out and slumbering near the edge of the forest, they carefully removed the clothing and hung it out to dry.

"Okay," I said, relenting. Life was too short to worry about something like this.

Someone scratched on our front door, and I flinched. I really didn't want to see who it was but avoiding Crall wouldn't make him go away. Rising, I flicked back the panel.

"Hey," Piper cried, stepping inside. She gave me a quick hug. "I stopped by to see if Missy wanted to come play and stay through dinner. You could also come to dinner if you want. Garek went foraging, and he brought back the most unusual tubers. He insists they taste like steak, though how he knows what steak tastes like is beyond me. We're going to grill them—his words—and I've made my own version of spicy barbecue sauce to slather all over them." She grinned.

"That sounds amazing," I said, turning to my daughter. "What do you say, Missy. Want to go to Noah's after we've finished helping Durran?"

Piper's eyes lit up. "Durran? What are you helping Durran with?" Her eyebrows wiggled.

"*Missy* and I are helping him with a trundier pup."

"Laylee's my new best friend," Missy said, swaying back and forth. "I'm gonna ride her."

Please, no riding. "Slow down, there. There's plenty of time for that."

"We've gotta go," she said, darting around Piper and out onto the decking. "Come on, Mom! Oh, hi, Durran."

Durran was here! My panicked gaze met Piper's.

"Go," she said with a smile, but tapped my arm as I

passed her, bringing me to a stop. "And anytime you want to take a walk in the woods with someone… You know, to stop and smell the flowers, you just let me know. I'll take Missy for an afternoon or a night, or even a week if you want."

My body hummed as I remembered his mouth sucking on me until I splintered around him. Despite not knowing his feelings, I wanted to do it again, a billion times, actually.

"You're way ahead of yourself," I said, feeling melty.

"Just so you know."

Smiling, I shook my head. After smoothing my t-shirt down over my hips, then my hair that was always a wild nest on my head, I stepped outside with Piper.

"Hi," I said to Durran, feeling suddenly shy. I kept picturing him kneeling between my legs…

"Greetings, Rayne," he said in a deep voice that made my skin tingle. Did he know what he did to me?

"Hi, Durran," Piper said. "How are the hatchlings?"

"Doing well. I anticipate the final three eggs will hatch soon."

"I bet they keep you busy."

His gaze never left me. "They do."

"Well, okay, then. I'll see you later, Missy?" Piper smoothed Missy's hair.

"Yup." Missy raced down the walkway toward the first platform while Piper went in the opposite direction.

Durran nudged his head for us to follow Missy, and we walked together. We passed a cluster of Ferlaern males who stopped and watched me. Their expressions remained respectful but after Crall, I was wise to feel nervous.

We left them and continued walking. Missy danced and twirled like a tiny ballerina. We arrived at the nesting grounds, and Missy waited for us beside a few buckets containing what looked like sludge.

"Grab one," Durran said to Missy. "If you are going to care for your trundier, you must start with her nutrition."

Missy poked the slimy surface of the substance. "What are we feeding her, mud?"

"It is boiled furstest broth."

She peered up at him. "What's a furstest?"

"Furstest is a mix of tubers, leaves, and the bones of a slunkette."

She blanched. "Bones?"

"For a trundier to grow strong, she needs lots of good food, rest, and activities that make her muscles grow stronger," I said, as I learned in my biology classes.

"That is correct," Durran said to me with a flash of his tusks.

Knee weakness time. My heart fluttering, I grinned up at him. Despite how sappy it sounded; I could get lost in his eyes.

When Missy tried to lift the bucket, I strode forward and took it from her. "I'll carry this."

She pouted. "Then what'll I carry?"

"Do you wish to take this?" Durran said.

I turned to find him flopping a dark purple lizard-like thing over his shoulder.

"Um, no," Missy said. "What are we gonna do with that?"

"You'll see," he said. His gaze fell on my hair. "You still wear my crustian."

I carefully touched the beetle clipped in place. I was tempted to remove it earlier, afraid I'd damage it, but wearing it reminded me of Durran. "I like it."

He flashed his tusks, and his attention shot to the trees. "Any news to share?"

"Yes." We fell into step together, walking behind Missy toward the nests in the back of the grounds. I shared what I discovered.

He stopped on the walkway, his eyes wide with wonder. "You already know the cause?"

Nodding, I bit my lower lip. His eyes followed the movement, and he gulped.

Just like that, heat smoldered inside me.

Focus!

"It's a plant," I said. "I have a fairly intact leaf I can show you later, if you'd like to come to my domit after dinner."

"I can do that."

My heart skipped a bunch of beats. "Perfect."

"Tomorrow, while we are hunting, we can look around and see if the issue is localized or widespread."

"Yes, during our hunt," I said hesitantly. "I'm not sure I'm much of a hunter, though. I hope that's okay."

"Hunting will move things along."

"Move what along?" Did we discuss the same thing? He seemed extra eager to take me hunting, though I wasn't sure why. We didn't have to kill something to get together.

"You will see."

Vague, but pressing him wouldn't lead me to new answers.

"I'm looking forward to hunting," I said, just so he'd know I wasn't hesitant about this... Was it a date? I couldn't be sure. Maybe the Ferlaern hunted in pairs, one male and one female.

His tusks flashed again, renewing the spark of hope inside me.

"Good." He directed his attention to the walkway. We reached the far-right side of the hatchling grounds, and he stopped. "You can lower the bucket here."

"What are we gonna do with the lizard thing?" Missy asked in a voice filled with equal parts awe and horror. She strode closer to Durran and stared up at him. "Will she eat it all right now or are we puttin' some in the freezer?"

"She will eat some," he said, his gaze shooting to meet mine before flitting away. Even a simple gaze stirred something deep inside me. "I'll feed the rest to other pups who need a boost. They grow quickly at this age and their parents have a hard time keeping up." His thick brows lifted and there was a soft twinkle in his eyes when he stared down at Missy. She barely came to his knees, reminding me all over again of how large these Ferlaern warriors were.

I liked his size, though. It gave me a feeling of security, like he could shelter me in his arms, and nothing would ever harm me.

"Do you think you're brave enough to slice up this creature and feed it to a pup?" he asked Missy.

"Sure." She peered around. "Where is she?"

"Here," Durran said softly, nudging his shoulder to a nest ahead and on our right. "She's hiding in the secret part of Bledard's nest."

"Who's Bledard?" Missy asked as she scrambled up the wide branch.

I latched onto her dress and held her back. "Hold on there, partner." "Partner" fit in with Piper's new wild west theme. "We don't jump into unknown nests. What if Bledard isn't friendly?"

Durran dropped the dead creature onto the walk beside him. "Bledard is mated with Jorlorn, my bonded trundier. I do not believe she's eaten any Earthling younglings yet."

I groaned. "Yet, huh?"

He flashed his tusks shyly and I was reminded all over

again of how appealing this guy was. His teasing ways. His muscular build. And the sweet way he treated my daughter. He leaned in close to whisper. "She will be kind to Missy. Trust me with this?"

His scent flooded my senses, making my skin tingle. My clit tingled, too.

Hell. Why was I picturing his mouth there again? It was crazy. We were about to chop up a dead creature to feed to a hatchling. My daughter stood nearby.

I was completely crazy about this guy.

Actually, I was pretty sure I was falling for him, though I had no idea if he saw me as more than a friend with benefits.

From the smolder in his eyes, I got the idea he could tell I was panting for him already.

"Let her go," he said, nudging his head to Missy. He called out to my daughter. "Visit with Laylee, though you won't find her in the first nest with Jorlorn or Bledard. Climb over the back and you'll see a second hidden one. That's where I put her."

"Aw, cool," Missy said, rushing up the branch.

"We should follow her," I said, my voice low and husky. Frankly, all I wanted to do was jump Durran's bones. Would he let me?

"We will…later." He took my hand and tugged me farther down the walkway then led me up a branch to an empty nest.

The second we were hidden among the lush canopy; I was all over him. He held out his arms, and I leaped up and started kissing him without even a how do you do.

He groaned, and his mouth responded to mine, taking and giving back tenfold. His big hands roamed my back, and he grabbed my ass and pulled me fully against his aroused cock.

We were feverish with each other, tugging at clothing and groping beneath.

I slid my hands up his shoulders to the top and pulled him closer. Let him feel me, feel my need. Let him get a taste of my feelings. Unable to get enough, I devoured his mouth, taking all he had to give.

Our tongues glided together, two souls playing an evasive dance of drawing close and pulling back.

When I lifted my head, he flashed his tusks in a devilish way, making my bones melt.

"Before you, I'd never kissed anyone," he said.

"You haven't done any of this before?"

He watched me before giving a negative jerk of his head.

This big, brawny guy—the one who sucked me with such infinite care until I came all over him—was a virgin?

"They say practice makes perfect," I said slyly.

He frowned. "Practice?"

This could be why he fumbled with the relationship we could be building. He might not know how to take things from casual conversation to something more.

"If you keep practicing, you're going to bowl me over," I said.

"Then I must practice." His mouth caught mine again and when our tongues touched, we both groaned. We kissed, and fire licked up my spine. I wanted more, but I also wanted to show him how wonderful we could be.

I lifted my head, and he watched as I slid down his body then tugged at the fastener to his pants. Pausing, I looked up at him. He nodded, giving permission, and I unfastened and spread his pants. His engorged cock sprang free.

Yessss…

It was big and wide and thin strands the width of

pencils and the length of my fingers wove around his golden dick, wiggling toward the tip like separate beings. One undulated near the base and I wondered how it would feel during sex. Would it hit my clit exactly where I ached to feel it?

Durran gave me the best orgasm of my life. It was time to return the favor.

He watched me raptly while I dropped and leaned forward.

Grabbing his cock with two hands, I licked the tip. He tasted amazing, like a spice I never sampled but would come to love more than any other.

Releasing muffled groans, he wove his fingers into my hair and held tight. His eyes closed as he gave into his bliss.

It was all I could do not to smile. No laughter, though it was time to have fun. There was something wildly freeing to know I was the first to taste him, to give him this satisfaction outside of whatever he'd done for himself.

I sucked as much of him into my mouth as I could, my tongue teasing along the strands that wiggled and stroked my teeth. These would feel amazing inside me, but I would wait. When we finally came together, and I had a feeling that time was "coming," I wanted to be alone with him for more than a few stolen moments.

I needed him for a full night. Maybe I should take Piper up on her offer of taking Missy so I could have alone time with Durran.

My body hummed, and the vibration transmitted to my mouth as I ran my tongue all over his cock.

He pumped toward me, his body tightening, his hands cupping my face and shoulders.

I loved that I could do this for him.

"Rayne," he moaned, his hips straining forward.

His cock tightened, and I sucked harder, gliding my tongue across the tip with each pump.

Moving faster, I mimicked the motion I ached to feel between my legs.

"Touch yourself," he commanded.

I couldn't resist. I unfastened my jeans and shoved them and my underwear down and stroked my clit before pushing my fingers into my wet folds.

As I sucked his dick, he shuddered and jerked, his body tightening, straining.

I worked myself into a frenzy.

"Come for me, Rayne," he half-shouted. "Imagine me buried deep inside you, my culier strands stroking your inner walls."

I'd never done anything like this before. Sure, I found satisfaction when I was alone, but I hadn't done it in front of someone else.

I sucked harder on Durran's cock while rubbing my fingers across my clit then dipping inside my slick folds. My hips jerked as I coiled tight.

His tail teased the back of my neck, coiling around, though not tightly.

All I could picture was him bending me over and impaling himself to the hilt before pulling out and plunging deeply all over again.

With an achingly beautiful shudder, I came, my body jerking.

"Yes," he whispered. "Like that." He wrapped my hair around his hand and held me close, and his muffled groan echoed around us.

As his seed shot into my mouth, another groan hissed from him, a glorious thing.

My body jerked again, succumbing to yet another orgasm.

I swallowed then licked the tip of his cock.

He eased backward, and we straightened our clothing.

Then taking a cue from his prior behavior, I stood and tipped my head toward the walkway. "Perhaps it's time to cut up that lizard?"

14

Rayne

He helped me climb down the branch to the walkway. My feet landed with a solid clunk. Would we continue as we were, finding feverish moments alone without mentioning what happened?

I wasn't sure how I felt about it other than loving the outcome.

One of these days, we'd need to talk about where this might be heading, but was there anything wrong with taking each moment as it came without analyzing what it meant?

Voices echoed from nearby, telling me we wouldn't be alone for long. I ached to drag him back into the nest for another round.

"Laylee's hungry," Missy said, her head poking over the nest. "I led her around and around until she was panting so she's gotta be stronger. Can we feed her?"

With a quick flash of his fangs my way, Durran dropped down beside the lizard and pulled a blade from a hilt at his waist. "Watch me, youngling," he said. "If you are going to care for a hatchling, you must learn everything."

She joined us on the walkway, her hand jutting toward the knife. "Let me do it?"

I struggled not to gape at my daughter. She'd never been squeamish but gutting a lizard was a little different from squishing an ant.

"Watch this time," he said as she sat next to him. "Next time, you will do it." With infinite care, he explained each part of the process.

I leaned against the rail and watched them together, struggling not to see this as a bonding moment between them. It would be unfair to start dreaming of Durran taking a father role with my daughter. He might not want something like that. She would, though, and I couldn't bear to see her hurt if things didn't work out between us.

Work out between us… I was assuming there was an us.

Maybe a new us. We'd been intimate. We were working together to save the clan's trees and Laylee. We were growing closer. This had to be leading somewhere. I came here to form a relationship with a Ferlaern. Why not Durran?

He cleaned the dead creature, placing bits of meat on two big leaves, then washed his hands in a bucket. After cleaning his knife, he returned it to its sheath and folded the leaves to make packages. After handing one to Missy, his head jerked toward the nest. "Let's climb up. I'll show you how to feed Laylee and leave the other package for Jorlorn's hatchling."

I followed them across a big nest at the top of the branch, gazing wide-eyed up at the enormous trundier perched on the side. It watched us with a benign expression that sharpened when we went near its hatchling.

When we left the valley weeks ago, I watched Durran

fly this beast, and they were a thing of beauty mid-air. If I asked, would he take me flying with him sometime? I rode with one of the other warriors to the valley, all the time longing to be in Durran's arms.

As Jorlorn's pup gobbled up the meat, we climbed over the back side of the nest and parted a thick curtain of canopy. If I didn't know this nest was here, I'd never suspect its hidden location.

We found Laylee cheeping in the middle. Squawking, she flapped her fine, lacy wings. I could almost hear her little belly growling with hunger.

"Here you go, honey," Missy chirped. She stooped down in the middle of the nest and unwrapped the leaf then watched while the baby waddled closer, her tiny beak extended. Her silky black, scaled body gleamed like a deep-earth diamond in the muted sunlight. She teetered on spindly legs.

Missy lifted a hunk of meat and the hatchling delicately plucked it off my daughter's palm. "That's right. Eat it all."

Laylee gulped the meat down without chewing, her neck straining as she swallowed the bulge. She moved forward, squawking.

"She likes it," Missy said with a grin. "She's getting stronger all the time."

I watched in amazement as the pup gulped down the meat, eating what had to be her own weight in food. When she finished, she turned a sleepy look Missy's way.

"Aw, you were hungry, weren't 'cha?" Missy said. Laylee sagged against Missy's side, and my daughter put her arm around the creature half her size. "Are you getting sleepy now that you have a full belly? I do that all the time."

Laylee collapsed against Missy's leg with a heavy sign.

The creature's eyes sagged before sliding closed, and a small snort rumbled in her throat.

"She's snoring," Missy said, beaming up at us. "I love her."

My throat tightened, and I leaned against Durran. His hand dropped casually onto my lower back, but his fingers stroked my spine.

I was rapidly becoming addicted to Durran.

Missy wiggled backward until she could lean against the side of the nest with Laylee lounging on her lap. "Come on, sleepy girl," she said. "You sleep and I'll keep you safe." She turned eyes shimmering with tears my way. "She's eating. She ran around. Does this mean she's growing strong?"

I dropped to my knees, gathered them both in my arms, and rested my chin on top of Missy's head. "I hope so, honey."

Missy sobbed. "I don't want her to die." She curled into my chest.

Durran stooped down beside us, his face wracked with grief. His hands reached out, and he hesitated before tugging the three of us into his arms. Sex was all well and good, but a kind, caring male offering the comfort of his embrace couldn't be beat.

My daughter slowly stopped crying. She suppressed a yawn and her eyelids dropped.

Durran eased back to look down at us. "I'm sorry," he whispered, but it wasn't his fault. He was as worried about this as I was.

"We'll find a way," I said softly. "Together."

He nodded, and when his eyes met mine, I read something there I couldn't define. Something warm and lasting. If I could reach out and capture it, I would, but it was as elusive as Durran.

After shifting us off his lap, he held his arms out toward Missy, who'd fallen asleep.

"I could carry her back to your domit." At my nod, he carefully took Laylee and settled her on a slice of fur tucked into a shadowy corner of the nest where the edge curled forward. Unless someone was looking specifically, they might miss her. He covered her with leaves.

This was a safe place to hide her but was it enough to fool Horesk?

Durran eased Missy from me and cradled her against his chest. She sniffled and sighed but didn't awaken as he slowly made his way toward the walkway.

Before stepping through the canopy veil, I peered back at the sleeping pup. Would she grow strong enough to avoid being culled? I hoped so and not only for my daughter's sake. Everything deserved a chance, even a tiny hatchling.

Durran led the way, holding Missy in such a gentle manner, it made my heart ache. I needed to stop wishing he could be a permanent part of our lives. He might not want that. We reached my domit and I led him inside and up the stairs to Missy's small room.

Stooping down beside her bed, he carefully laid her on the quilt I brought with me from Earth, shifting her back and forth to ease it out from underneath her.

I made the blanket myself, though I was no seamstress. Each night, I stitched together the patches I cut from clothing Missy outgrew, plus a few of the maternity tops I wore while pregnant with her. Each piece contained a bit of our past we brought with us into the future.

Durran spread the quilt over Missy, and she sighed and curled onto her side. He stroked her hair then turned to give me a gentle smile. Again, I read something undefined in his eyes.

If only…

I reminded myself—again—I would not try to grasp something that wasn't mine, but it was getting hard to remember why I took such care to protect my heart.

If he held out his hands, I'd hand it over willingly.

Creeping from Missy's room, we went downstairs.

"Thank you for carrying her back," I said, keeping my voice low. While Missy could sleep through a rocket launch, an ache was growing in my chest, and it felt natural to speak in low tones.

I was falling for Durran but I had no clue what to do about it. Love was a wonderful feeling, but it hurt when my love wasn't returned.

"I'll see you tomorrow after breakfast?" he asked at the door.

"Yes. It won't take long to look for evidence regarding the trees. This will leave us plenty of time for hunting." Missy would spend the day with Noah.

Teddy nudged the lower corner of the flap open and sauntered inside.

"There you are, baby," I said, scooping her up and cuddling her against my neck. Her purr rumbled through the room, louder than a tiny creature should be able to produce.

Durran rubbed her ears and neck, and she leaned into his touch. With a flash of his tusks toward me, he shifted the door flap to the side and stepped out onto the walkway.

"Tomorrow," he said as the flap slid closed.

He was gone before I could reply.

15

Durran

Early the next sunslice, I watched Rayne's domit until she and Missy left for breakfast. Then, with anticipation building inside me, I put the next part of my courtship plan in place.

I joined them in the dining domit, sidling into the room and filling a plate with food then waiting to approach her until she saw me. She sat with Garek, Piper, and Noah, plus a few other warriors crowding close, hovering over Rayne's every word.

It was all I could do not to cringe. She didn't want to eat with me. She was happy talking to other males. Maybe I should take my plate to my domit.

Her arm fully lifted. "Durran!"

Conversation ceased in the large domit, the occupants sitting at ten or so other tables stopping whatever they were doing to turn and look my way.

Now I really wanted to bolt. But Rayne smiled and the excitement in her eyes drew me to her. I crossed the room. As I approached, she waved to the other males and said something I couldn't make out. The three shot me scowls

and the ones sitting at her side got up and strode toward
the entrance, leaving only two behind.

"Sit," she said, patting the newly created space
beside her.

How could I refuse her command? I lowered my plate
onto the table and joined her, sitting so close our thighs
brushed.

My skin caught fire like it always did when she was
near. Did she feel the same?

She leaned near and spoke only to me. "Missed you."

Wait. She did?

"We're spending time together this morning," I said as
if that was the right answer. I had a feeling it wasn't.

The remaining males—contenders—sitting opposite us
scowled.

"What are you doing this morning?" one asked, recov-
ering. He directed his question to Rayne, and I awaited her
answer. Would she brush our arrangements aside casually
or give them merit?

Courting Earthlings was very complicated.

"We're going hunting," Rayne said cheerfully.

Garek, sitting to the side of the warrior, grunted. His
tail flicked up behind him. "Hunting?"

My back spiked. "It is a worthy tradition."

"Indeed." He leaned forward and crooked his finger to
tug my head close. Piper continued to help Noah with his
breakfast, though she shot me a sympathetic smile. "If you
need advice..." Garek said.

My skin prickled. "I do not." Fuck. Could Rayne hear?

He slapped my shoulder, an Earthling gesture I'd seen
friends use, though I still didn't understand why. "You
know where to find me."

I did, but I already sought advice from Narcial, and I
intended to follow it.

"Thanks," I mumbled.

One of the males, Nigest, engaged Rayne in conversation while the other tried to interject his own comments into whatever they discussed.

I stared down at my plate, wondering if I had an appetite left. What if she wanted to go hunting with Nigest instead of me?

To occupy my hands, I picked up a sliver of toonen and bit off a hunk, chewing slowly. I fiddled with the slice of munjeer bread then lifted it and pushed bits of it into my mouth until I finished. Then I pushed my plate back.

"Are you done?" Rayne asked. At my nod, she stood, juggling my plate, as well as her own and Missy's. "I'll take these up and be right back. Do you have anything you need to do before we leave? Also…" She glanced down at her dress. "I probably need to wear something else, right?"

"Pants would be more suitable." Though I did enjoy looking at her legs as she moved. And with a dress, I could tug it up if she seemed receptive. "Wear the dress, though."

"Dress?" Nigest said with a hoot. "Who wears clothing like this on a hunt?"

"I guess I do," Rayne said pleasantly but even I read the hint of steel in her voice. Don't mess with this woman or live to regret it.

"Oh, yes, of course," Nigest said, backtracking. He lifted his plate and fumbled it, nearly dropping it on the floor. "You look lovely in the dress." His gaze shot to mine and the pleading there almost made me come to his defense. *Almost.*

Rayne took the plates to the return table and left them.

"I'm ready to go, then," Rayne said brightly when she got back. She turned to Missy. "I'll see you at Piper's later, honey?"

Missy barreled into Rayne's side for a hug. "Yup. See ya' later!" She whirled and ran around the table to join Noah.

"I guess I'm all set, then." Rayne's smile grew. I'd rather cup her face and kiss her than take my next breath. "You're ready?"

"Yes."

We left to chimes of goodbye.

Outside, she stopped on the walkway. "Where would you like to meet up to go hunting? I have a few things to collect in my domit, mostly sample things, though I thought I'd bring my magnifying glass just in case. But for hunting, is there anything specific I need?" She flared out her skirt. "I'm still not sure this is the most practical get-up for hunting but if you like it, I'll wear it."

"You look lovely." My appetite may have fled but I wanted nothing more than to kiss her. Lick every bit of her body.

"Thank you." Her face pinkened. "You look pretty good yourself."

I brushed my hands down my chest. "I wear what I always do, pants and my weapons."

She leaned in close. "And as always, you look hot."

Hot was a good thing. I learned this from Piper, having asked after I overheard her telling Garek he was hot.

Rayne thought I was sexy? Well, she *had* licked my cock. It was happy to remind myself of the event from the moment I woke until I feel asleep at night.

"So, about half an hour?" she said.

"How long is that?"

"Thirty minutes."

Munette was essentially a minute, from what I also learned from Piper. "That sounds perfect. I'll come to your domit?"

"All right." With another sunny smile, she left, walking across the walkway in the direction of her home.

Since Horesk's domit was a few platforms beyond Rayne's, I followed her. I wanted to see if he returned but I was also eager to see the results of my latest courtship venture.

I couldn't stop thinking about Rayne's mouth surrounding my cock. I'd never imagined her doing anything like that and now I wouldn't be able to dream of anything else.

Did she like me? I had no way of knowing.

I supposed I could ask but asking meant laying yourself out in front of someone. It meant being vulnerable, something I avoided since my mother died and my father rejected me.

No, I would keep doing things for Rayne, showing her what I could offer, and when I was confident she felt the same, I'd… Well, I wasn't completely sure what I'd do, but I'd figure it out then.

As they approached her domit, Rayne's pace slowed.

I slowed my own pace.

Rayne stopped on the walk.

I stopped, too.

"Are you following me?" she asked, and I tried to read her mood from the tone of her voice.

I wasn't good at this courtship thing.

And I wasn't even sure Rayne and I were courting.

"I'm not exactly following you," I finally said. "I'm…" Think fast. "I'm walking this way, so I decided to accompany you to ensure you reach your domit safely."

A peek over her shoulder showed her eyes sparkled with humor. My tight gut loosened. "If you're going the same way, why not say so and walk with me? It's not like we're strangers."

"You are correct. We're not strangers." I strode up to her, and she tipped her head back, her gaze meeting mine.

"We're friends, right?" she said.

"We are friends."

She winked. What did that mean? "We're actually friends with benefits."

Benefits… Oh, did she mean the spontaneous things we did together? Frankly, I looked forward to each interaction, wondering what we'd do next.

"Friends with benefits can walk together," she said, and I fell into step beside her. "At this point, there's absolutely no reason to be shy."

"Is that what you think I am?" I was. I was.

The thin lines of facial hair above her eyes lifted. "Aren't you?"

"I am cautious," I sputtered.

"Why?"

"I…" Did I dare share? Trust wasn't easily given, but this was Rayne. I gave my body to her not long ago, and it was the most amazing experience in my life. "I have scars."

"I think they go deeper than your skin."

"You're perceptive."

Stopping on the walkway, she waited while a group of Ferlaern males strode past. Each paused to dip his head her way, their gazes flicking between us. They wondered why I was near her. Why she was near me. If we were together or passing each other with no intention of speaking.

I wanted to take her hand and pull her into the shelter of my arms. I wanted to show the world she meant everything to me.

They continued on, leaving us leaning against the rail, our arms brushing but without me sheltering her in my arms or declaring anything.

Narcial was right. If I didn't make my intentions known, someone else would. Rayne did things with me. The beneficial friendship things. They were wondrous and exciting and perfect. I wanted to keep doing them with her, to show her I could be creative and spontaneous as well. I wanted to claim her.

But did she want to be claimed?

"Your scars are just your surface, Durran," she said softly. "And for what it's worth, I like what I see."

"They're ugly." *I* was ugly.

"Only to someone who can't see who you are beneath. Don't you know? I see."

Narcial mentioned this.

What would it be like to fully let down my guard with this female? If I let her in, she could hurt me.

If I didn't let her in, it was guaranteed I'd be hurt.

"Who did this to you, Durran?" she asked, fully facing me. She leaned in close, and her arms went around me as if *she* were the one doing the claiming. "I'll happily kill them for you, if you want."

My laugh snorted out, loosening my mood. I tugged her fully against me, showing her how much my body wanted her. How much *I* wanted her.

"I am a grown warrior. I protect myself," I said.

"Is there any harm in letting someone stand beside you while you do it?" Her words were muffled against my chest, and her lips tickled my scarred skin.

Was there? It would be nice to face life with someone beside me.

No, to face it with Rayne.

But I had to woo her first. Show her who I truly was. I would follow the elder's suggestions and only then Rayne would wish to be my mate.

"Hey, Mom. Hey, Mom!" Missy ran toward us with a big grin on her face. "You're not gonna believe it!"

Rayne broke out of our embrace. Did she wish to hide whatever was going on with us from her daughter?

"Piper and Noah came with me so I could change into pants, and something happened to our domit," Missy exclaimed.

"What happened?" Rayne pressed her clasped hands against her chest and reading fear there hit me like a kick in the gut. Just like I worried about caring and being rejected, I assumed Rayne worried about losing the bit of security she found here in our village. "Is everything okay?"

The shake in her voice sent me to her. Fuck friendship benefits. Fuck my fear of her turning away. She needed me and I would be there for her. I wrapped my arms around her and held her, showing her she was not alone.

I wasn't the only one who ached for someone to stand beside me while we faced whatever the world flung in our direction. Rayne did, too.

"It's nothing bad, Mom." Missy hugged Rayne's leg from the side. "It's… It's flowers." She grabbed her mother's hand and pulling her out of my embrace, tugged her in that direction.

"What do you mean flowers?" Rayne shot a look over her shoulder I couldn't interpret but it lit my bones on fire. "Do the domits bloom more than once?"

"They do not." I hurried after them, eager to be there when she saw what I'd done.

It is all right, I wanted to say to her. *You will be happy.*

"Slow down, Missy," Rayne said with laughter in her voice.

"You've gotta see!"

We arrived at her domit, and I hung back, watching.

My heart thundered in my chest as anticipation took hold and swept me up into the sky along with it.

Rayne pushed the door aside and gasped. She backed away, and the door flapped closed again.

"Did you…" She looked to her daughter but shook her head. "Of course, you didn't do that. You were with us."

Piper stood nearby, grinning but saying nothing. Noah must be with Garek.

"Hey, Rayne," Alexa said, walking past, holding the hands of her two youngling sons. When I asked, I was told they had just turned three-cycles-old. "Hot day, huh?" She paused and swiped the light-colored hair off her face. The rest hung down her back.

Her sons fidgeted, trying to kick each other.

I lifted one up and placed him on my shoulders. He squealed with excitement and immediately tried to grab onto a branch overhead. I worried if he latched on, he'd swing up and I wouldn't be able to get him down.

"Did you do it?" Rayne asked Alexa, a big grin spreading on her face.

"Do what?" Alexa asked, latching onto the back of her second son who was attempting to stand on top of the railing. "We don't climb the rails, Benjamin."

"Did you flower bomb my domit?" Rayne asked. "They're gorgeous. I'll feel like I'm swimming in flowers, and I imagine I'll have to toss some of them out so I can walk around."

"Flowers?" Alexa asked with a frown.

Piper chuckled, glancing at me.

"Yeah, look." Rayne opened the door again, showing off my handiwork. "It's…amazing."

I couldn't stop from flashing my tusks. My crustian was well received as were my flowers. After going hunting, she wouldn't be able to resist me.

"That's…something else," Alexa exclaimed, sidling close to the door. "Amazing." Her gaze shot to me before returning to Rayne. "You didn't do it yourself?"

"What? No. I was at the dining domit."

Alexa rolled her eyes as Ben flopped on the decking on his back and proceeded to kick the railing. "I didn't flower bomb your domit, but someone did." She nudged my side with her elbow. "Do you think one of the other guys did it, Durran?"

Alexa's son leaned over and bit my horn, and it stung, but I smiled, extricated him from it, and returned him to his feet.

Earthling younglings were a challenge.

"Females enjoy flowers, do they not?" I asked pleasantly, trying not to give anything away with my face.

"Women do enjoy flowers," Alexa said. "Maybe not a billion of them, but they smell pretty, and they cheer up a domit."

"It is too many." My sunny mood fled. Had I overstepped or done this incorrectly?

"Nope, I think it's just the right amount," Piper said. She tapped her chin. "Now, I wonder who gave them to you, Rayne?"

"I know, I know!" Alexa said, lifting her hand. "He's standing quite close to you."

"Did you do it?" Rayne said, and I could only nod.

"I, um…"

"I actually stopped to ask you two if you've seen Bruge?" Alexa asked, maybe sensing how awkward I felt. I expected to be alone with Rayne when she discovered my courtship gesture. "His trundier arrived last night and someone told me he had a meeting with Garek. I've looked everywhere but can't find him."

"He returned to his clan not long ago," I said. He

helped me pick and bring flowers from the forest floor after I waylaid him as he was walking to the platform to fly home. His snickers still rang out in my mind. He was also curious about Earthling courtship customs and speculated about employing some of the older Ferlaern traditions.

I tried to dissuade him from the idea of kidnapping one of the females—he didn't say who—but I didn't have much success. In past cycles, Ferlaern males would steal a female (after ensuring she was somewhat willing) and take her to a hidden location where he could use his every means of persuasion to convince her to mate.

Alexa's face fell. "Oh. He's gone? That's too bad."

Was Bruge interested in Alexa?

"Would you like me to send him a message?" I asked, assuming this would be helpful.

"Sure," she said. "Tell him…" Her growl slipped out.

My hand reflexively went to a weapon. I peered around, seeking the threat, but saw nothing but leaves fluttering in the breeze and branches swaying. And one of her sons hanging from a branch beyond the railing. I reached out and grabbed him then returned him to the decking.

"Oh, thanks," Alexa said. "Ben, what did I tell you about leaving the walkways? Remember? It's dangerous. You could fall. You could be hurt. Stay here with your brother, okay?" Her gaze flicked to me before she scurried after her second son, grabbing the back of his shirt before he darted around the narrow band encircling the outer edge of Rayne's domit. "Boys. Stop. William? Benjamin? I'll only tell you once. Stop." She returned to the walkway with a son's arm in each hand. "I need harnesses. I know that would horrify every parenting blog out there, but I can't be chasing them all day long."

"We have domits where Ferlaern mothers used to take their youngling during the day."

"Truly?" Alexa danced on the walkway. "You have daycare domits? I've died and gone to heaven."

"Where are they?" Rayne asked. "Then I won't have to bug Piper all the time to watch Missy."

"I don't know if they're active any longer," I said. "The females who ran the program died from the disease."

"We could set up a cooperative," Alexa said with enthusiasm. "Take turns. And while we're at it, we could give the kids lessons. Unless there's a domit school here."

"Not any longer," I said.

"I'm sorry." Rayne rubbed my arm. "We all lost so much to that wretched disease."

"So, schooling and daycare," Alexa said. "I'll talk to Garek about using the domits but perhaps the best way to handle this is to set up a meeting with everyone involved. We can discuss options and come up with a plan. But…a daycare!" She wiggled her hips. "I'd just about kill for a daycare. Just one hour. Ten minutes! I'd be able to think. Bathe. Sleep. Breathe."

"What would you like me to tell Bruge?" I asked.

"Actually, don't tell him anything." Alexa hauled her son up off the decking again and took his hand. "I'm heading to the dining hall. Want to join us for breakfast?" She snorted. "Actually, want to join us while these two throw their breakfast? Dining with us is an adventure."

"We already ate, and I have flowers to arrange," Rayne said. "Then I'm going hunting."

Alexa frowned. "Hunting? What do you plan to hunt?"

"I'm not sure," Rayne said. She looked to me and closed one eye, smiling. What did one eye closing mean? She did it earlier. Did she have something in her eye? "Maybe I'm hunting one particular Ferlaern."

"Oh." Alexa grinned. "Well, I wish you good luck with it. Come on, boys. Let's go see if they have pancakes." She dragged her sons down the walkway. "No pancakes, but maybe something similar? Meat. You guys love meat. Let's go eat meat."

"So, I'll see you in a few minutes—munettes?" Rayne said with a chuckle.

"Thirty."

She saluted, another odd gesture.

I nodded and started down the walkway that would take me past Horesk's domit. I would finish my errands and get back to Rayne as soon as possible.

Rayne watched Alexa wrangle her younglings across a nearby platform. "And I thought Missy was a handful."

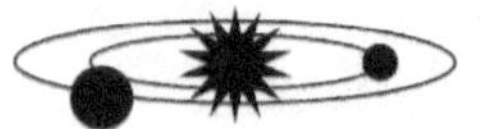

Durran

I found Horesk sitting on a bench outside his domit, and my gut clenched as I approached.

He looked up and scowled.

Not pausing for social niceties, I stopped in front of him and jumped right in.

"I want you to give me one moon to help Laylee get stronger," I said firmly. I added my hands on my hips to show him I was serious.

Inside, I was still a youngling asking for what should be freely given.

"Laylee?" he asked in a crotchety voice that told me his patience was limited. Nothing unusual there. He peered up at me with lifted brow ridges. "What is a laylee?"

"The small trundier pup is named Laylee."

"It's a mistake to name a creature such as that."

"She's strong. Healthy."

"It is weak. It needs to be dolced immediately." With a growl, he rose and tried to brush past me.

I grabbed his arm but released it when his fierce glare sliced through my skin. Not truly but it felt like it.

"Fewer pups hatch each year," I said. "We need to foster them all, including those we would've dolced in the past." Not me. I never dolced a pup; Horesk did it while I cringed and didn't intervene.

Why had I held back?

Because I still hoped this male would see my value, that he wouldn't reject me like he rejected the smallest hatchlings.

Was I truly that weak?

No, no, I wasn't. I never had been, and that realization gave me the strength to stand up to this surly male I lost respect for cycles ago.

"I should never have let you dolce any of them," I said.

"It was not your decision."

"The practice needs to change."

He sneered. "It is not your decision." His finger gouged his chest. "This is my role in this clan. Yours is to feed the trundiers and clean up after them."

He said it like I should be ashamed of what I did here, but I wasn't. I loved working with the trundiers and helping younglings find their perfect match among the hatchlings.

"One does not need to wear a powldron to be strong," I said.

"You can't even do that right."

"You are the eldest. It was never my role to take the Willen powldron." Yet I would do it when I was called.

Horesk stiffened. "There is honor in being an elder. My brother was very happy to become the clan's warlord." His chest puffed. "And I have been very happy serving this clan as elder instead."

He brought me here when I was young, leaving his brother to take over the leadership role when their father died. If I'd remained with my uncle, would he have treated me differently than my own father?

"Go clean a trundier, youngling, and leave the dolcing to me," he said with a snarl, trying to shoulder past me.

Only now did I realize his approval no longer matter. What had changed?

I had. My confidence had grown since the Earthlings arrived—since Rayne joined our clan. Her acceptance of who I was both on the inside and out meant so much more than Horesk's snide opinion of a youngling he should treasure as his own but instead chose to throw away.

Horesk grumbled. "If you were better at your job, we'd hatch more pups."

"I don't control the breeding or egg laying," I said. He would blame me for something I had no say in?

Well, he'd done the same when my mother died, blaming me. I was six; she fell from a cliff. He was the one who should've been there for her. There was no way I could've saved her.

But rehashing the past would not bring her back. It would not make this surly elder respect me.

"I ask for time to help Laylee get stronger," I said. "As the favor you owe me."

He cricked his head, intrigued while still maintaining a look of amusement on his wrinkled face. "Why do you think I owe you a favor?"

"Because you've done nothing for me my entire life. Do this one thing."

His hands fisted at his sides. "I gave you life, and that was enough."

"Mother did that, not you. You were nothing more than her mate, and not a good one at that." Memories of them yelling and of her sadness after he left crashed through me. His status as an elder always came first.

Would he have treated her differently if she were his maelstrom mate? It hardly mattered. She fell and died, and he continued to pursue the future he envisioned, leaving me behind. I essentially raised myself.

"I'm glad to hear you agree," he said sardonically. "I don't owe you anything." He stomped away from me but stopped on the wide platform to turn back. "I want you to dolce the pup. Show me you can be more than just a lowly trundier trainer. Do something strong, something that will make me proud."

How would killing a defenseless creature make anyone proud?

"I will not."

"As I thought." Turning away, he strode to the wide platform before stopping again. This time, he didn't turn back. "Do it or I will handle it myself. You have one sunslice."

17

Rayne

Someone scratched on the door. After what happened with Crall, I needed to be careful. I lifted the stick I found on one of the platforms and brandished it as I wove through the lovely carpet of flowers covering my living room floor. They smelled heavenly. I wasn't sure how long they'd last, but I'd treasure them until they faded solely because they were given to me by Durran.

I flicked the door flap back.

Durran frowned at the stick I held aloft. "Is there a problem?"

Should I tell him about Crall? I was tempted. But I also wanted to have fun today with Durran, not spend the day going over what happened.

I'd tell him later.

"Nope," I said, lowering my arm. "I had this handy in case a…liscard was at the door."

"You think a liscard will scratch at your door?"

"You never know, do you?" I said breezily. I tossed the stick onto the sofa and grabbed my small pack, securing it on my back. "I'm ready. How about you?"

"Perhaps you'd prefer to have this instead of a stick if a liscard comes… scratching at your door." With a flourish, he presented the short sword I borrowed from him the other day when I went down to the ground to investigate the trees. "This has been repaired and it's yours."

"Oh, cool," I said, taking it from him. "It's really pretty."

"Swords are not pretty. They are mighty and fierce." He fisted his chest in a manly way and flashed his tusks, showing me he was teasing.

"It's still pretty."

"This is yours as well," he said, holding out a sheath. "Allow me?"

At my nod, he knelt in front of me and fastened it around my waist then slid the blade into the pouch. He looked up at me and in a flash, I wanted him.

His nostrils widened, and his pupils dilated. "Rayne," he whispered.

I dropped the door flap behind him, shutting us inside my domit.

We tumbled to the floor amid the flowers, tugging at each other's clothing. He bared my breasts and latched onto a nipple with his mouth, gliding his tongue across the tip.

A moan burst from me, and I arched toward him. He continued to lick my breasts while I writhed.

His hand cupped me between the legs, and I panted with need.

His fingers fumbled with my dress, dragging it up to my waist. The sword clanged against the floor, falling out of the sheath, and he nudged aside a cluster of extra-pesky flowers. Grunting with excitement, he shredded my panties then kissed his way down my body. He spread my legs wide and licked me from the bottom to the top.

My spine jolted with need, and I bucked upward while he sucked my clit into his mouth and carefully nibbled on it with his tusks.

With his fingers moving inside me and his mouth on my clit, I wouldn't last long. It felt exquisite. Blissful. Amazing. I gyrated against him like a feral creature, begging for more.

His tail got in on the action, the rounded, rubbery tip probing deeply. When it stroked my G-spot, I whimpered. My eyeballs rolled back in my head.

He hummed against my clit while his tail pumped.

And just like that, my body exploded in a ferocious orgasm. Durran continued to move his tail within me and lick my clit while I rode one wave after another, each more intense than the last.

Until I lay beneath him, a limp thing who could barely think.

Looking up at me, he grinned. "You like that."

"You could tell, huh?" I puffed out, a trembling mass of ecstasy. This guy made my brain spin, my lungs ache, and my heart shatter.

"Perhaps I am good at one thing," he said, pride shining in his voice.

I had a feeling my virgin alien lover would be good at a lot of things.

He backed away and stood, offering me a hand to help me up. In all honesty, I wasn't sure I'd be able to stand. But I took his hand and he tugged me up, his arms going around me when I stumbled.

"Your turn," I said, reaching for the fastener on his pants.

His fingers stilled mine. "No time, but later we can…" He shook his head and for a second looked uncertain. Did he think there wouldn't be more times like this for us?

At this rate, we'd be humping against a tree within an hour.

I so wanted some humping with Durran. I couldn't stop thinking about his cock. Those strands moving along the sides would feel amazing, and the one at the base that would hit my clit perfectly.

"Are you ready to go?" he asked, his mood overly sunny. I loved seeing a cocky side of Durran. He was so often shy and hesitant.

"I am."

I scooted into my room and put on new undies as mine were in pieces, and we left my domit, taking a vine down to the ground.

"Hunting or investigation first?" I asked softly, not wanting to draw liscards to us. "And what are we hunting?" Why were we hunting was another question, but I withheld it. He was running this show, and I'd follow. Besides, my bones were still melty from all those orgasms. This male had a magical tongue and a nimble tail.

"Let's hunt." He held out his hand and I took it. "As for what, you will see."

I wasn't thrilled at the idea of stalking prey then watching it bleed out, but I was thrilled about spending time with Durran.

He led me along the path leading to the platform where the Ferlaern mounted their trundiers. When we climbed the stairs and stood on the level surface, he called out.

Jorlorn flew down from the heavens, screeching. He landed with a heavy thud and then stooped down onto his belly.

"Can you climb or would you like help?" Durran asked.

"I've only ridden a trundier a few times, just when we

traveled from the valley." I rode with an older warrior who was polite, though distant. The guy barely said a peep during the entire trip, only answering my numerous questions with single answers. I was focused on holding Missy and keeping her safe. The thought of her falling kept me a wreck for much of the journey.

What would it be like to fly in the arms of someone I loved?

Well, I was about to have that opportunity.

"Let me help you, then," he said, taking my hand and tugging me closer to the creature.

As we approached, Jorlorn's nose jutted forward to sniff me. I wasn't sure how to interpret the rumble in his chest but hoped this was his way of being friendly. When he didn't take a chunk out of my thigh but nuzzled Durran, the tension in my spine eased.

Durran's broad hands spanned my waist and with a quick lift, he seated me behind the spike, on Jorlorn's shoulders. I latched onto the spike and was reminded all over again how high off the ground these beasts flew.

"What does flying have to do with hunting?" I asked, not taking pride in the shake in my voice.

"You will see." One leap and he sat behind me. His arm went loosely around my waist as if it belonged there.

Actually, it did.

"Ready?" he said close to my ear. The rumble of his deep voice sparked through me and made heat pool between my legs all over again.

I nodded, unable to speak coherently.

Oh, hell, yeah, I was more than ready. But he didn't mean sex, unfortunately. Although, if I leaned forward and lifted my skirt…

Jorlorn sprang into the air, and the thought of sex and hot cocks pumping inside me fled in a flash.

I wasn't ashamed to admit an eep burst from my throat.

Durran chuckled, and his arm tightened around me. "Hold on."

To the spike. That was the only handle in sight.

I closed my eyes, but then peeped them open, taking in the ground dropping beneath us, the flap of Jorlorn's wings, and the heat of Durran sitting behind me.

Maybe this was going to be okay.

"As for hunting, we are after the fearsome drundest."

"What's a drundest?"

His free arm lifted. "See?"

A speck—no, a cluster of specks—appeared ahead, low on the horizon. No, they hovered above a spindly forest lining the side of a steep mountain peak.

I squinted but couldn't quite see. "Birds?"

"Not quite." I swore he was laughing. Why would he be laughing? "Do you have your weapon ready?"

"I have no idea how to use it." I fumbled to pull my blade, unsure what the hell I'd do with it if we were attacked by the drundest. I could brandish it, but it would be a struggle not to drop it if anything dove toward us.

As we got closer, I frowned, sensing a trick. "Wait."

"Wait for what?" he asked.

"They're not birds." Though I had no idea what they were.

"Watch." From his pocket, he pulled a dark, woven object. A flick of his hand and it spread out in a net. He nudged his thighs against Jorlorn, and the beast took a nosedive downward.

More eeps escaped my mouth, and I swore my lips peeled back from the rush of the wind. My hair whipped behind us, flaying Durran, but excitement crept through me, which took me by surprise.

"This is awesome," I shouted, releasing the spike with a jerk. I spread my arms out wide and let the wind buffet me, knowing I was completely safe with Durran's arm wrapped around my waist.

"You are amazing," he said, kissing my neck. "Rayne."

When we got close to the drundest, I could see they were somehow attached to the trees.

"They're not alive," I cried out. "We're not going to stab anything and make it bleed!"

"We are not. They live but are plants. Fruit of the drunder tree, actually. Quite tasty."

"So are you."

His chest expanded, and I swore he sorta gurgled.

"You choking back there?" I asked, straining to turn enough to see.

"I am fine. Rayne. One of these sunslices…"

"I'm ready. You pick the time and place."

He kissed the back of my neck again and guided Jorlorn closer to the mountain. As we skimmed above the trees, he dropped the net. A jerk, and he hauled it in, laden with drundest.

"Hunting, huh?" I said with a laugh. "You had me going there. I thought we were going to stab an alien bunny then skin and gut it. I can't imagine why you'd choose to offer me this activity, but I was willing to go along."

"I appreciate that."

The confidence in his voice buoyed me, making my heart sing and my pulse flit around in a rapid patter. If we were on the ground, I'd be ripping at his pants despite his suggestion of "later".

He turned Jorlorn and flew back toward the forest housing our clan, and I leaned back against him, savoring how good it felt to be close to him. I wanted to do this always.

Jorlorn landed on the platform and Durran slid down the beast's side, landing lightly on the ground. He lowered the bundle of drundest and held his arms up to me.

I had no problem flinging myself off the trundier, knowing full well Durran would catch me.

He eased me to the ground and stroked my hair back off my face. "We'll share the drundest with the clan if you want or we can hoard them for ourselves."

"I'll try one and let you know." I had no problem sharing, but it was fun to imagine us sneaking around eating them like it was our own special secret.

He tugged one free of the netting and handed it to me like it was a precious gift.

But then, it was.

It came from Durran.

Yummy fruit consumed; we took the bundle to my domit. It tasted amazing but I couldn't hoard it all; I'd bring the bulk of it to the dining domit tonight and share it with everyone else. I couldn't wait for Missy to try it.

We returned to the forest floor, and I followed Durran down a path leading in the general direction of the trees I needed to examine.

He stopped at the very same tree. "What experiment do we need to do?" he asked. His gaze flicked down my body, and heat rumbled through me again. But I wasn't sure we dared the distraction. I didn't want Durran eaten by a liscard while he was eating me.

Focus on the trees, Rayne.

The sizeable bulge in his pants drew my eye. I wanted to feel that inside me, more than just about anything.

"We, um…" What was I going to say?

He grinned and it was clear he was thinking. I wanted him and he knew it. Our needs were in sync. "We um…?"

I closed my eyes to block him out and made my brain think of anything but his cock. It sure wasn't easy. With Durran, I was insatiable.

I nudged my head toward the forest. "I want to look around the trees and verify if the plant I discovered is natural or…"

"Or if it appears someone is purposefully leaving it here," he finished.

"Yeah." I opened my eyes and looked at the tree. At least it didn't have a hard on.

I needed to think of something other than sex.

Leaving him, I walked around, examining the ground closely. On the opposite side, I found a place where the ground had been disturbed, though it wasn't the same location where I obtained my sample. "What's this?" I whispered, stooping down.

Excitement sparked through me.

"What did you find?" Durran stooped down beside me.

"I'm not sure yet. It could be nothing." Pulling my trowel from my pack, I carefully scooped out the soil, digging down beside the wide roots of this mighty tree. About six inches below the surface, I came to a place where a hole had been widened. It was full of the same plant I discovered in my samples.

"Do you recognize this?" I asked, tugging a clump out and handing it to Durran.

"It's frylar weed. What's it doing in the hole?"

I shrugged. "I think it was placed here. The hole is stuffed full of it."

"Its toxin leaches into the soil and kills the trees."

"Yeah."

"Someone deliberately put it here. There's no other way to look at it."

My nod came out jerky. An ache in my chest wouldn't go away. "Why would someone do this?"

"I have no idea, but I will find out." Durran stood, his face grim. "Let's look at the other trees."

We worked our way through this section of the forest and were dismayed to find each tree supporting our canopy home was being poisoned with frylar weed.

"I didn't know this weed could kill trees. Someone discovered it can harm trees and deliberately placed some at the roots. From the freshness of the clump we found at the most recent tree, I'd say they're coming here regularly and adding more weed."

"We need to find out who it is." Sadness made my bones spasm. Why would someone want to destroy our way of life? I leaned against the tree and patted it, trying to let it know I'd do something to save it. "We need to tell Garek."

"He can post more guards."

"Not guards," I said with anger bursting inside me. It shoved aside my dismay and took charge. "We need to set a trap to catch them. "

"Good idea." He frowned.

"And once we find out who it is…"

"They'll pay."

18

Durran

We returned the earth beneath the trees to how it was before and took a vine to the decking above. Wasting no time, we went to Garek's domit and filled him in on our find.

"You're right," Garek said, nodding slowly. "We need to trap this person. This is why you will one day take your uncle's powldron and it will fuse to your shoulder." He stroked his own that he wore always. It had finished melding to his skin and while I knew he removed it when he slept at night, it was a living part of him during the day. He said it enhanced his strength, but that couldn't be true, could it?

We walked to the door.

"I'll set this up immediately," Garek said. He smiled at Rayne. "Thank you for looking into this. If you hadn't…" He shook his head.

"So scary," Piper said, hugging Rayne. "I'll see you tomorrow?"

"Sure," Rayne said. She called out to her daughter. "Time to go, Missy."

Footsteps sounded overhead as Missy crossed the room. She bounded down the stairs and joined us, yawning while she leaned into her mother.

"I'll let you know how it goes," Garek said to me. He reached out and banged my shoulder, using the same supposedly friendly Earthling gesture. Each time he did it, I braced myself for an attack, though I well knew one would never come from my friend.

Someday, I hope to feel warmth when he did it.

After, Rayne, Missy, and I walked to their domit.

She shifted aside the door flap. Sunlight streaked across the sky in pink and gold tendrils. Leaves rustled overhead and if they weren't fading, I'd believe the trees were as healthy as always.

"Would you like to come in?" she asked softly.

Missy stumbled through the opening. She snatched Teddy off the floor and held her close while the creature purred. It reminded me of my own gressler pet and how much I missed his company. Perhaps I should adopt one my own.

I wanted to accept Rayne's offer; I craved to love her body all over again. But her daughter was here, and I'd monopolized her day already.

"Another time?" I said, watching her face. "I want to check on Laylee."

"I'll go with you," Missy said, crowding in between us.

Rayne's eyebrows lifted. "Oh, I don't think—"

"She could come with me if you don't mind," I said. I hadn't spent much time with younglings, but there was something precious and sweet about Missy. She made my heart ache as much as Rayne.

"I guess there's no harm in it. I could do a few things around here." She shot me a nervous smile.

"I will keep her completely safe," I said, pressing my fist against my chest.

"Oh, I'm not worried about that. I know you will." She stroked Missy's hair. "Have a fun time with Laylee and Durran."

Missy darted out through the door opening. I bravely leaned forward and gave Rayne a kiss. Couldn't help it. I wanted to touch her all the time.

She stood among my courtship flowers, stunned, while I stepped outside.

"I'll see you tomorrow?" I called out. "Would you like to bring Missy after breakfast to work with Laylee again?"

"I'd love that." She stepped out onto the decking, and her arm went around her daughter's shoulder.

"Could I speak to you for a munette, Rayne?" Crall asked, striding up from the end of the walkway.

A shadow passed over her face, and my spine jolted. I don't know why I did it. It wasn't natural for me to be territorial. But I tugged Rayne close and wrapped my arms around her.

She sighed against my chest and looked up at me. "I don't have time to talk, Crall. Can't you see I'm busy?"

He grumbled and glanced back and forth between us before storming toward the platform connecting this one to others.

"Are you having problems with Crall?"

"He's been a bit pushy, but I can handle him," she rushed to say.

I glared at the male's retreating back. "You don't need to handle him alone."

Her arms tightened around me. "I appreciate it."

"I'll talk to him if you want." I could also bash his head in whether she wanted me to or not. She trembled, which told me he frightened her. Anyone who even looked at her the wrong way needed to feel my wrath.

"Will talking to him help?"

"I'll tell him…" To leave her alone or he could face me. That would work. I might be a "lowly trainer," per my father, but the other Ferlaern respected me. I was handy with a weapon. "You will not need to worry about him any longer."

Tension left her body, and she eased away from me. "Thanks. I'm not sure how this sort of thing is handled here."

"Come on, we gotta hurry," Missy said, jumping up and latching onto one of my fingers. She tugged me toward the platform.

A glance over my shoulder showed Rayne smiling as she watched us walk away together. She went inside while I focused on Missy.

I'd never considered having younglings before; I never thought a female would look my way long enough for it to happen. For one munette, I could imagine what it would be like to have a child look up at me as Missy did, with wonder and excitement.

"I'm gonna play with her and kiss her and tell her a bedtime story after we feed her." She paused on the walkway and frowned up at me. "You don't have a lizard to feed her."

"I have meat nearby we can use."

"Oh, good." She started skipping down the walkway again, pulling me along behind her. Her hair danced around her head and when she smiled, she reminded me of Rayne.

I steered Missy the long way around so we could pass Crall's domit. When we got close, my pace slowed. I stopped in front of his door. If Missy weren't with me, I'd speak to him now. Instead, I leaned close and listened, determining he was inside. Good. I hoped he stayed there long enough for me to find him once I'd finished with Laylee and returned Missy home.

We continued on and arrived at Jorlorn's nest. I retrieved the packets of meat I'd set aside for tonight, and we clambered up the branch. As I fed Jorlorn's hatchling, Missy scrambled over the back side and into Laylee's nest. The small creature's coos soon reached me, making me grin.

I followed and found Missy tossing a small stick across the nest. Laylee scampered after it, plucked it up in her beak, and brought it back to Missy. They played until Laylee sagged against the child.

I sat beside her, and we fed the creature who seemed to make gains every munette. I hoped it would be enough.

No, it would never be enough. Was this hidden nest enough to keep Horesk away from the hatchling? It had to be. I couldn't take her into the mountains, and there were no other secret locations.

Once Laylee finished and fell asleep on Missy's lap, Missy leaned against me and sighed. "I like it here."

"With Laylee?"

"That but here on Ferlaern. I like our domit, my friends, and…I like you, too, Durran." She looked up at me with such wonder it made my heart still. "Will you be my friend, too?"

"I would be honored to be your friend, Missy."

The wind picked up and swept her hair around her face. She pushed it off, but it swirled around again.

"Would you braid it like Mommy does?" she asked.

"Braid?" As in, create a weave with the strands?

"Yeah, you know. Braid it. Mommy sometimes makes a crown. Can you do that, too, Durran?"

"I don't know if I can weave a crown, but I can try to…braid it, if you'd like."

She wiggled around until her back faced me and held up her hand.

I stared at her fingers until she peered up at me. "Take it."

"Take what?"

Younglings were a great mystery.

"The hair tie," she said, waving her arm in the air.

Hair tie…

Ah. The thin band around her wrist? I tugged it over her hand then examined it, marveling at how it stretched. "What is this made of?"

She shrugged.

It hardly mattered. But… It was a treasure to be watched over. Imagine all the things one could do with something like this.

"Braid me," she said. "Don't forget the crown!"

I was to turn her hair into a crown? Hmm.

The strands were silky and slipped through my fingers when I tried to scrunch them up onto her head. I wasn't sure where the hair tie would come in as I couldn't get her hair to remain in place.

"You have to take the strands and braid them," Missy said politely. This youngling had patience an elder could emulate. "Let me show you."

Rising to her feet, she went around behind me and started sorting my hair into bands. "You make three and do this."

I couldn't see, but I could feel the tender care she took not to tug my hair as she twisted and turned it, crafting one long band hanging down my back.

"Do you have a hair tie?" she asked.

"Just this." I held up hers.

"I tell ya what. I'll let you use this one and when we get back to our domit, Mommy will braid my hair and fasten it with another."

"You have more than one?" I marveled.

She leaned around to look at my face as if she suspected I was teasing. "We have a whole bunch of them. Don't you?"

"I do not."

"Aw, okay, then. You can keep this one. The pink goes good with the purple parts of your hair." She sighed. "Wish I had purple in my hair. My friend back on Earth, Jenny, her mom let her put purple dye in her hair and it looked good. But when I asked Mommy, she said no." She dropped the secured band of my hair onto my back and came around in front of me. "Would you ask Mommy if I can get purple dye so my hair can be like yours?"

I did not know what dye was and if it involved death, my answer would be no. However, I could learn this crown braiding technique as I'd like to spend more time with my new friend, Missy. Making crown braiding would be my first adventure.

"I'll talk to her about...dying of the hair, but I can make no promises," I said.

"That's okay." She yawned and peered around me at Laylee. "She's so pretty sleeping, isn't she?"

"She is." I stood. "We should let her rest, don't you think?"

"Yeah. I should go home, too. Mommy will be missing me."

We hid Laylee under the overhang, covered her with leaves, then left, walking toward her domit side-by-side. Again, I wondered what it would be like to have a child of my own.

A youngling like Missy.

She wasn't of my blood but did that matter? The heart chose, not the flesh.

"Why don't you have any kids, Durran?" she chirped, looking up at me with such innocence, it almost ripped my heart out. Pray no one ever stole that from her, that sweet, open, kindness found only in a child.

"I haven't mated yet."

Yet? Had I truly suggested there was a chance I could be mated in the future? With Rayne, it was hard to think of anything else.

"I think you'd be a good dad," she said, taking my finger and holding tight.

My heart pinched. "Thank you."

When we reached her domit, Rayne stepped outside.

"Have fun, sweetie?" she asked, kissing the top of Missy's head.

"Yeah." Missy yawned. "I forgot to tell her a bedtime story, but I will tomorrow."

"We can tell her together," I suggested, having no idea what kind of story I could make up. I used to be solidly grounded in my day-to-day life. I never dreamed.

Missy hugged my legs. "I love you, Durran."

Rayne's lips trembled, and her eyes shimmered as she watched us.

I patted Missy's back. "I...love you, too, youngling." How could I not?

"Thank you," Rayne mouthed. A tear trickled down her face.

She took Missy's hand, and they went inside together.

I walked slowly toward my domit; I had no problem coming up with fantastical dreams of what life might be like with a family.

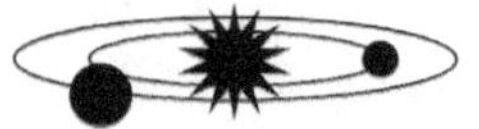

19

Durran

Early the next morning, I headed for the bathing domits. Ages ago, our ancestors started migrating between the lowlands in the south for the balmy winter moons and then the mountain valleys to escape the heat of summer. When we began bonding with trundiers, we settled in the canopy to give us easier access to them. The blossom domits worked perfectly for homes. We only had to move every other winter to a new blossom before the old one dropped from the canopy.

Bathing in the river snaking through the valley worked well, but we discovered if we channeled water from higher elevations and heated it before releasing it into a series of large domits, we could privately bathe no matter what the weather was outside. Within each bathing domit, we built large pools that took up much of the inside surface.

Finding most of them full, I worked my way down the walkway, looking for the signal beside the door that would show it was empty. Near the end, I located a bathing domit with no marker. I nudged the door aside and stepped into the darkened interior.

"Oh," someone said as my eyes adjusted.

Rayne stood thigh-deep in water, completely naked.

I must be dreaming. I rubbed my eyes but when I looked again, she remained in front of me, all her delectable flesh exposed.

The bag containing my clean clothing dropped from my hand, thudding on the membranous floor.

"I'm sorry," I backed toward the door, smacking into the wall instead. I couldn't drag my eyes off her body, from her pert breasts to her soft belly, to the triangle of hair between her legs. I'd seen the latter. Shifted it aside to taste what was hidden beneath.

I wanted to glide my tongue across her slit again and nibble on her clit.

"I'll leave," I half-groaned. Fumbling with the door flap, I turned away.

"You don't need to go." Her alluring voice called to the deepest, most hidden part of me. The vulnerable part only she could reach.

My hand stilled on the door flap.

"Can you tell me something, Durran?" she asked.

I didn't turn. Couldn't turn. "What would you like to know?" How could I speak normally? She was *naked*. Desirable. Someone I ached for with everything inside me.

"The crustian beetle you gave me." Hesitancy came through in her voice as if she were as unsure about this as I was. That couldn't be true. She exuded confidence. "Was the beetle intended to be part of a courtship ritual? *Your* courtship ritual?"

I gulped and my throat closed off. What if I said it was and she rejected me? It would hurt, and I wasn't sure I could bear the pain.

"Durran?" she asked with only kindness in her voice. "Was it?"

If I said nothing, if I walked away, I'd never know her thoughts.

Suddenly, I found myself filled with an overwhelming need to hear what she had to say.

"It was," I croaked out.

"You want to court me?" she said, her voice lifting. Did I hear excitement or dismay? I couldn't tell, and I wouldn't know unless I faced her.

Faced my fear.

I didn't know much, but one thing was clear. I didn't want to run from this female.

Turning, I was male enough to admit my knees shook. "I do want to court you."

My shoulder stung and I winced. Had I been bitten? I rubbed where it hurt but basically ignored it after that. Nothing could keep my gaze off Rayne, not even the fluttering in my chest.

"And the flowers?" she asked in wonder.

"Yes, the flowers, too. Someone told me giving flowers was an Earth courtship custom." If—a big if there—we came together, I wanted to combine both our worlds as we'd combine ourselves, fusing Earth and Ferlaern traditions.

"Flowers are something couples give each other back on Earth." Her soft, sweet laugh tinkled through the room. "Usually it's a small bouquet, though, not filling an entire room."

"I insulted you?" Fuck. I hadn't thought of giving only a few. I wanted to do something grand, something that would show her how big my feelings were for her.

"I wasn't insulted at all." A swallow worked its way down her slender throat, and I traced the movement with my eyes. "And hunting? Was that something couples do together here?"

"That, uh, is a Ferlaern courtship tradition like the crustian."

I was totally revealed. How would she respond?

"I had a lot of fun," she said, her fingers trailing back and forth through the water. "It was a perfect date."

Date…? Oh, yes. My translator suggested this was a fruit but there was more than one meaning for the word.

Dating also meant establishing a specific timeframe of an event.

No, not that.

It was a way of stating someone was old-fashioned, a term I was also unfamiliar with.

I doubt she meant that.

The final definition suggested it was a way of building a romantic relationship.

I preferred that meaning most of all.

While I pondered the wonder of a date with Rayne, she held out her hand. "I want you to court me. I want everything, Durran, but I need to know if you feel the same or if all this has been only…friends with benefits."

"Everything, everything?" I asked, taking a step forward. How could I deny the entreaty in her voice?

"I've tried to show you how much you mean to me with my gestures, though I admit it's been sexual and nowhere near as sweet and seducing like your beetle and flowers. And what I've done to your body," she chuckled, "few would call it honorable, though I guess it's not dishonorable either."

"Was my hunt—date—successful?"

"Very much so," she said in a bubbly voice. "I think you caught what you intended to—me." She moved toward me until she reached the edge of the pool. Water glided down her body and I wanted to lick off each drop. "Tell me, Durran."

"Tell you…?"

Back in her domit, I sought permission before I spread her legs and sucked and licked her until she found pleasure. I could put aside this uncomfortable conversation and do the same thing. She'd enjoy it. I'd enjoy it.

But how long could we keep doing things like this without discussing our feelings? It was scary laying myself out for her to view. I'd be exposed.

Who better to expose myself to than Rayne? That realization sank through me, soothed me. Actually, it gave me wings. If I wanted, I could soar all the way to the moons, and I had a feeling Rayne would be there at my side.

"Tell me if you want everything, Durran, because I have to know. I've been hurt in the past. I gave myself to someone I thought would treasure me always, but he didn't. It broke my trust because our entire relationship was dishonest. He wanted one thing and once he had it, he tossed me aside. I'm not sure I could bear it if you did the same." Her voice shook. "No, I know I couldn't bear it. It's not the same at all with you, though. I cared for him, but I… I love you."

I stepped into the pool fully clothed. Nothing and no one would keep me from touching this precious female.

"You love me?" My voice shook. The wonder of this munette sunk through me, filling me up in a way I'd never been before.

Biting her lower lip, she nodded. "I do. I always will."

"Rayne," I sighed, my heart pinching tight.

She held up her hand. "If you're going to reject me, do it now and make it quick. Like pulling off a Band-Aid. Rip it free and leave me. I'll deal with the pain alone."

"You'll never have to deal with anything alone again if you want to have me in your life."

"I think that's all I've ever wanted, Durran. Just you and whatever you want to give me."

I pressed my clasped hand against my chest then held it out to her like I had the crustian. Like my flowers. Hunting. Each gesture was a tiny piece of me I offered tentatively enough she could turn it away without causing pain.

It would always hurt if she rejected me. So much more than when I was a youngling and my mother's death was followed by my father spurning me.

Rayne cupped my hand in both of hers then leaned forward to kiss it. "If I open your fingers, what will I find?"

"All of me, Rayne," I said in a deep, throaty voice tight with emotion. "All of me."

She gently pulled my fist apart then pressed the open palm against her chest. "Can you feel my heart beating for you?"

I did. It encompassed me in a way I never experienced before. For the first time, I trusted someone not to hurt me.

Her gaze glided down my front. "I think you're overdressed, Durran."

I gaped down at my saturated clothing. "I believe you're right, mate."

"Mate?" Joy and wonder filled her voice. "You want me as your mate?"

"I do. I love you, Rayne. I always will."

"Durran." Tears sprang up in her eyes, but she beamed with a smile that filled my bones with joy.

She tugged at my clothing, ripped at my clothing, tossing the items aside, until I stood before her as naked as she. Her smile was so bright, it shone like the two moons above when they were full. The stars even.

Everything that was beautiful in my world was wrapped up in this female.

"If you'll have me, Rayne," I said. "I'll be your forever mate for as long as you want me."

"Then you better get used to eternity."

20

Rayne

He loved me, and I needed to show him I felt the same. Words were one thing. They were simple to use and too often thrown aside when they were no longer convenient.

Expressing my love—making a memory of my love—would last forever.

I stepped back into the deeper water, tugging him along with me. I hadn't forgotten he'd never had sex before, and I'd never take this moment lightly. But I wanted to show him how wonderful it could be.

In one way, I was in virgin territory myself. I'd never made love with someone I cared for as much as Durran.

He watched my face, his smooth and relaxed, without a hint of concern in his eyes.

"I want you completely, Durran," I said.

"I feel the same."

I loved how deep and husky his voice was. How engorged his cock was, too, but I'd get to that.

"I don't know what I'm doing," he said. "Not completely."

"Have you jerked off before?"

"Jerked…?"

"Pleasured yourself with your hand."

He nodded.

"Then you've got a basic idea. It's different being inside someone just as it is when a woman takes a male inside her body for the first time. Sometimes, it's over fast."

"I have…jerked off many times," he said with a low laugh. "I have seen how quickly it can be over."

"Have you experimented with making it last longer?"

"I have."

One of these days, I wanted to watch. Would he open himself up enough to do that for me? I'd ask, though not today. It was time for us to be together.

"I assume guys use the same idea to make things last longer when they're inside a female. It's silky in there. Wet." Especially now. I might be the one getting off fast. I ached deep inside for him. I needed to feel him heavy and fast, slamming into me until we both exploded. "I just don't want you worrying about how long it lasts or if we're together at the end."

My first time with my boyfriend was truly awful. He was big, though nothing like the Ferlaern who seemed universally huge. He pushed hard, and it hurt mostly because of his size. It was so uncomfortable; I wasn't even sure he was all the way in. I asked—an embarrassing moment right there. We did it a few more times, and it got better, though it was never wonderful. He didn't care about my needs.

I wanted more than better with Durran, but I was patient enough to wait until we were in tune with each other's bodies.

"You are saying it is all right if I don't give you full pleasure," he said with a frown. "That will never do."

"I'm sure you'll give me pleasure one way or another. I just want you to know that if I don't orgasm, it doesn't mean I didn't enjoy it."

"Oh, you'll orgasm."

Confident and cocky but he was still a virgin. He hadn't done it, and he wouldn't know how it would go until he was deeply seated inside.

Hell, I wanted him there right now but there was no harm in a little foreplay.

I dropped down and cupped his enormous cock with both hands. It was silky, even the culier strands. One coiled around my finger and I almost came at the thought of what it could do inside me.

"Rayne." He wove his fingers into my wet hair, gripping my head tight. His muscles strained, and his voice deepened, which didn't seem possible.

Leaning closer, I licked the tip of his cock then pulled the head into my mouth. I wished I could take all of him but that was impossible. I wasn't even sure all of him would fit inside me, though we'd sure as hell try.

I sucked in as much of him as I could. My tongue flicked the tip each time I eased back, and his groans filled the bathing chamber.

"Rayne." He held my head and tugged his hips back. "I want…"

"I know what you want. I do, too." I looked up at him and made no attempt to hide my feelings. They blazed on my face for him to drink in. "Let's see how it goes, okay?"

He lifted and carried me over to the outer wall where they built a shelf. Lowering me onto it, he followed, dipping down into the water while spreading my legs.

His mouth descended and like the time before, his clever tongue worked me to a fever pitch while his tail teased. I writhed as he flicked my clit then pushed his tongue deep inside me.

"Durran. Now." My voice came out deep and guttural. Need consumed me, and I ached for the bliss that would follow.

He eased himself up and over me. "This way?" he said, placing the head of his cock at my opening. "Or… There are other positions."

I loved a guy with an imagination but maybe this position would work well for a first time. The culier strand at the base of his cock would hit my clit perfectly.

"Yes," I said simply. I lifted my legs up, though my heels barely reached his shoulders. He had a new mark on his right shoulder… I shook my head. I'd look later.

"I want…" His palms landed on the decking on either side of my shoulders, and he captured my mouth. His tongue dove inside to entwine with mine, and a moan worked its way through me.

I jerked my hips up, aching to feel all of him.

"Impatient mate, aren't you?" he asked, his voice full of tease. "Never fear. I plan to give you everything you need."

"Give it to me now," I whined.

"Like this?" He pushed forward, only partly seating himself inside.

The stretch was exquisite, and I nearly came.

"Yes," I said, my eyes on his.

He watched me, watched my movements and expressions as if he needed to memorize this moment. After pulling back a bit, he drove himself forward again, this time pushing all the way inside.

"Man," I hissed. "That's…"

He stilled, waiting.

"Wonderful. Awesome."

A grin filled his face, highlighting his tusks. "It is, isn't it?"

"There's more," I said slyly.

"I bet there is. Like this?" His hips pulled back, and he thrust forward again.

"More, Durran." My fingers tightened on his arms as a wildness filled me. I was on fire and only he could extinguish the flame.

I'd prepared myself for fumbles. For it being over so fast I barely knew he was inside. This was anything but. We both knew our bodies and what gave them pleasure. Now we discovered that pleasing the other was even better.

He moved in and out, pushing hard with each thrust. The culier strand at the top of his cock glided across my clit each time. It had a slightly ribbed underside that rocked my core and built my need to a thrashing storm.

With a quickened pace, he rocked hard against me, his body pummeling mine, driving me across the smooth surface.

He buried his face in my neck, and his tusks grazed my skin, pinching on my right shoulder. "Mate. You are mine."

I was. Completely, and I reveled in the feeling, savoring the push and pull of his cock driving deeply. The culier strands nudged my G-spot with each thrust, and some near the tip stroked my deep inner walls. It was an indescribable feeling and I wished it could last forever.

My body rose higher, until I could almost touch the stars.

Durran's muscles strained as he went even faster. Cords stood out sharp in his neck, and his face reflected his bliss.

I thought… Hell, I was foolish to think this guy wouldn't give everything he had to me.

I couldn't hold myself back. I spiraled tighter, higher,

until I burst, my body shuddering and my inside quaking around him.

He grunted and with a groan, shoved himself to the hilt, filling me completely. His body trembled; his muscles quaked.

And he came deep inside me.

Things changed after that, as they usually did when a couple got intimate. We spent our days helping him with the trundiers and playing with Laylee, secure in the belief she was hidden well enough she'd be safe until she was stronger.

We hadn't seen Horesk and that was fine with me. The evil dude could remain locked in his domit forever, as far as I was concerned. He hadn't come after us to reinforce his one sunslice edict, and it weighed on me. Hopefully, she was hidden well enough he couldn't find her.

At night, after Missy went to sleep, Durran crept into my bed. We were voracious, barely able to keep our hands off each other.

It was how it should be. Nothing would ever pull us apart.

"I want to tell Missy, if that's okay with you," I said while lying in his arms six nights later. "I've never... I mean, I went out with guys back on Earth, but I never brought them home to meet her. But..."

"But?" he said by my ear.

"This isn't solely my decision. It's yours as well. I don't want to push you or make you feel you need to commit to me if you're not ready or if," how I could even think this after all we'd done together was beyond me, "if you aren't ready for this kind of relationship."

"Mate," he said, stroking my arms. "I want every-thing." His fingers teased across my belly and dropped down between my legs to glide across my wet slit. He fastened onto my clit and rolled it while his tail teased my opening.

We'd barely finished, and he wanted me again. Could life get any better?

As he rose over me and pressed the head of his stiff cock between my folds, he whispered by my ear. "Tell her I want to be a part of her life." His words thrilled through me. "That I want both of you in my life forever."

I woke the next morning to someone scratching at my door.

"Durran," the male called out, anger lifting his voice.

Durran growled and his arms tightened around me before they loosened, and he eased me off him.

Early sunlight sliced through the small window near my bed, piercing the space between us.

"Durran! Get out here."

Horesk.

"What do you think he wants?" Unreasonable fear jolted inside me. "Do you think he found Laylee?"

I leaped from the bed and tugged on a dress then yanked my hair back in a ponytail while Durran hauled on his pants.

"I don't believe he did," he said, though his grim tone was mirrored on his tight face. He started for the door but paused. "Maybe you should wait—"

"We'll face him together," I said with the strength of a thousand Earth women.

He took my hand and kissed it.

We walked to the door, and I mentally girded myself. Why was he here and what did he want? I couldn't believe this was a friendly social visit.

I tugged back the door flap and stepped outside so close to Horesk he reeled backward. Good. He needed to be on his guard with me.

"What do you want?" Durran asked pleasantly, though a thread of unease edged into his voice. He crossed his arms on his chest and his hand teased along the hilt of a knife.

"How dare you be here with her!" Spittle flew from Horesk's mouth, and he gnashed his tusks. His hands clenched to fists and I backed away a step, worried he'd strike. I should've brought my sword, though I wasn't sure it was a good idea to gut a clan elder.

"You have no say in this Horesk," Durran said blandly, his arm going around me, tugging me close. "You gave up that right long ago."

Did the elder have a say in everyone's relationships? I hadn't heard that from my friends. But this guy tried to break up Piper and Garek. Maybe he wanted to break up me and Durran.

Evil bastard.

"Of course, I have the right." Horesk stormed up to us, fury almost crackling in his graying hair. He poked Durran's shoulder, and my eyes were drawn to the mark.

A maelstrom mark.

My breath caught, and I pushed aside the sleeve of my dress, finding a matching symbol on my own shoulder.

Awe spread through me. "We're maelstrom mates, Durran."

His eyes widened as he took in the symbol I showed him.

"No!" Horesk bellowed. "As your father, I forbid this!"

"Father?" Backing away, I gaped at Durran.

I had to admit, I was hurt. Why hadn't he told me something as important as this?

Guys always lied, didn't they?

For a moment, I gave into the insecurity roaring through me. It was tainted by my past experience.

This was the same way I felt when my boyfriend stopped taking my calls. When he sent a message saying he'd pay child support, but he wanted nothing to do with the child. *Your* child, he called Missy as if he played no role other than sperm donor.

He didn't want me. He never wanted me. He wanted sex and I gave it.

My skin flashed over with sweat, and my mouth went dry. My chest ached and the spiraling feeling wouldn't go away.

While the males argued, I turned and stared at the trees, realizing we still didn't know who poisoned them. Would I research that alone then return to my lonely domit, moving on with my life like I had when my boyfriend ditched me?

Clutching the railing, I closed my eyes.

But then they blazed open.

Hell, no.

No matter what, I knew Durran loved me. If he hadn't told me about Horesk, he had a good reason. He'd explain, and I'd understand.

I loved him, and that wasn't going to change.

I turned to face Durran—to tell him I believed in him. Believed in us.

But he—and Horesk—were already gone.

21

Rayne

I wanted to chase after Durran, but my daughter was inside my domit, asleep. If she woke and I was gone, she'd be scared. What if Crall came by?

I didn't trust him.

So, I went inside and sat on the sofa, staring forward blindly, hoping Durran would come back. We'd talk. He'd explain, and I'd understand. I was determined to understand why he didn't share this with me.

He didn't owe me anything. If he chose to keep a secret like this to himself, it was his right. But the elder wanted to harm an innocent creature. He appeared determined to keep Earthlings from matching with the Ferlaern. Wouldn't Durran tell the woman he loved pertinent information like that?

Teddy climbed up onto my lap and purring, coiled into a little ball and fell asleep. I stroked her soft body, feeling bad for only half paying attention to her.

"Time to go see Laylee," Missy chirped from the top of the stairs, jolting me into the present. I was so absorbed in what happened, I didn't hear her moving around upstairs.

She skipped down the stairs and ran over to give me a hug. "Missed you, Mommy."

"Missed you, too, honey," I said, holding her tight. I wasn't sure why my eyes kept tearing. I had no reason to cry. "Let's go get some breakfast and then we can go to the hatchling grounds, okay?"

"Okay." She danced over to the door, full of more energy that I'd be able to drum up on any day in my life. Actually, I felt kind of dreary.

Crap, I knew why.

"I need to get dressed first," I said, looking down at the nighty I'd thrown on when Horesk snarled at my door. I rose and tugged on shorts and a t-shirt then followed her down the walkways to the dining domit. Inside, we filled plates with food and sat with Piper and Noah.

The kids chattered about everything from riding trundiers to going down to the ground to look for gresslings.

"No!" Piper and I shouted at the same time, sharing a shudder.

"Promise me you won't do this," I said, holding Missy's arm and making stern eye contact.

"Why not?"

"It's not safe there. Stay up here in the canopy. Stay with an adult around at all times."

"But I go see Laylee," Missy said, frowning.

"Not alone, though, correct?" Please not alone and at night anymore.

"Not too much."

Ugh. "Also promise me you'll only go to see Laylee with someone else; go in a team." And take a machine gun with you, I chose not to add.

We intended to set up a school, so we'd do this sooner rather than later. The first lesson would be to address safety. Was there a way to teach our kids self-defense skills they could use against alien creatures? Maybe. I'd ask Durran.

Durran. Sigh.

I hadn't seen him in the dining domit and hoped we'd meet up soon. We needed to talk. I had a few things I needed to say, but they wouldn't be said in a scolding manner.

Missy and I finished our breakfast, though I didn't eat more than a few bites, and walked to the hatchling grounds. I was determined to act calm and collected despite my churning innards. I'd listen to what Durran had to say and I—dammit—would be kind and understanding, the way I'd want him to treat me.

"Durran?" I called out as we walked down the walkway with nests in the trees above and to both sides of us.

He didn't reply.

"Maybe he's with Laylee," Missy said, running ahead. She reached the branch leading to Jorlorn's nest and climbed it nimbler than a monkey.

I lumbered up behind her, nowhere near as nimble as a monkey.

Jorlorn was gone but that didn't mean anything. He could be hunting or off on an adventure. His mate watched us with intent eyes as I followed Missy across the nest and over the side to the hidden location.

Laylee chirped and raced toward us, and I swore she was stronger. My eyes stung because that meant she'd live. I hoped she'd live. The thought of Horesk culling her ripped me apart.

"We didn't bring her anything to eat," Missy said sadly. "She's hungry."

"How about this?" I said with a smile, holding out the

cloth wrapped with items I picked up at breakfast for the trundier pup, just in case. Unwrapping it, I revealed a variety of meats and even something the Ferlaern called waffles, though they really weren't anything like them. More…ground leaf waffles with tiny dents in the top. They tasted okay. No maple syrup, but this was a new world, not our old one.

I missed waffles.

"Oh, Mommy, thanks," Missy squealed, grabbing the bundle from me. She sat and the trundier pup clambered up onto her lap, straining to reach the food Missy held overhead. Missy laughed, the cheerful sound making me smile.

It was hard leaving Earth and bringing a small child to an alien planet. I gulped when I applied for the program. What would it be like? How would the Ferlaern treat us? These were just a few of the numerous questions I peppered myself with over the weeks leading up to our acceptance.

Missy was happy here. We had few worries. And it was nice living a relaxed life close to nature.

Would she grow up and choose to be with a Ferlaern or would one of the humans call to her heart? I didn't know but I was happy to be here with her while she took in all her new life had to offer.

I sat beside her, and the pup climbed into my lap and butted my chest with affection.

Laylee really was easy to love.

We returned to our domit. Though I still hadn't seen Durran.

Worry consumed me. Was he upset with me for turning

away if only for a few minutes? I didn't understand why he took off.

By late afternoon, I couldn't stand it any longer.

"Let's go for a walk," I told Missy.

"But I'm playing with Teddy," she said, sitting on the sofa with a piece of string held overhead while the tiny animal leaped up to catch it.

"We could stop by Noah's domit and see if he wants to play."

She pouted. "Noah's a boy."

"And that was okay this morning."

"Boys are yucky."

Okay. "He's your friend. That makes him not-yucky."

"Girls are everything sweet and spicy and boys are bugs."

That wasn't the way I remembered that phrase, but it was close enough.

"So, no playing with Noah?" I asked.

"Nope."

I wondered what he'd done to offend her, if anything at all. "Then come with me."

"I could stay here alone."

"No way. You're only five." Going on fourteen, obviously, if she was sweet and spicy. "It's Noah's or come with me."

"I could go play with Savvy."

Josie's thirteen-year-old daughter was everyone's favorite babysitter, possibly favorite because she was our only babysitter, being the oldest among the Earth kids.

"We could stop by Josie's domit and see if she's available—free, that is."

"Yay." Missy carefully lowered the now sleepy Teddy onto the sofa beside her and stood. "Let's go, Mom. Let's go." She rushed to the door flap and shifted it aside, bursting through the opening and out onto the decking.

Shaking my head, I followed.

We found Savvy home and she was happy to play with Missy. Poor kid didn't have any friends her own age, though she'd met a few Ferlaern teenagers. Thankfully, she was still happy to hang out with our kids.

I left the two playing with stick dolls, something Savvy probably rolled her eyes at, though she was indulgent to Missy. Missy was thrilled, however, and squealed with joy when Savvy suggested it. I promised to return after dinner to pick her up.

My first stop was Garek's office, which was really a small domit near the center of the village. Since the blossom was stunted, it only had one room. I scratched and slipped inside.

He wasn't there.

Hmm.

Leaving the office, I strode along the walkway, crossing two platforms. I was passing Narcial's domit when she came out.

"Oh, there you are," she said.

"Yes. I'm…here." What did she mean by that? No matter. "I was looking for Durran. Have you seen him?"

"Durran? He left." Her lips pursed.

"Left. Did he go hunting?" Meat for Laylee, most likely.

"No, he left for the Willen Clan."

"They're a few valleys away, correct?"

She gave me a pert nod. "You are correct."

"Why?"

"Why is the Clan a few valleys away?" she asked as if she really thought that was what I was asking.

"No, why did he leave?"

"Oh," she said softly. "You don't know?"

"Know what?" This was like pulling teeth.

"He was called home by his uncle who is eager to pass on his powldron."

Just like that?

I frowned, and for now ignored the "called home" part of her statement. "His uncle wants to give him his powldron? Garek wears one, right? It means he's the warlord of this clan."

"Yes, that is what I meant by powldron."

"But... Durran's a trundier trainer."

"He's also a nephew of the Willen Clan's warlord, and the warlord is eager to have Durran take over the clan."

Hold on. I grabbed her arm when she would've nudged past me. "He left?" My knees quaked. What if he didn't return?

"Yes, I just said that," she said kindly, patting my arm. "He's gone to the Willen Clan. Assuming the powldron accepts him, he'll remain there as their warlord."

"The leader of *that* Clan?"

She sighed. "Yes, the leader of that clan."

"But I don't want him to leave." I wanted to talk to him, be with him. I needed to explain that I wasn't rejecting him, but the look of dismay on his face haunted me. I was stunned. I backed away. And he left.

Why hadn't I seen this? He was rejected by his father, obviously. He was scarred, and from what I'd seen, Ferlaern females shunned him because he wasn't as "pretty" as the other males, though I thought he was gorgeous. And now he thought I was angry with him and turned away. He thought I rejected him, too.

"How can I get to the Willen Clan?" I asked with urgency lifting my voice.

"You wish to travel there?" she asked, reeling back in

amazement. Her feet stumbled on the walkway, but she righted herself.

"I do."

Her chuckle rang around us, and she came forward and gave me a gentle hug. "Dear Earthling female. If you wish to travel to the Willen Clan, I'll take you there myself."

22

Durran

My uncle dipped his head forward and lifted his hands, extending his powldron toward me. "It is time, nephew. This is yours and with it comes the warlord status of our Willen Clan."

I wanted this. I'd ached for this role my entire life despite my joy in caring for trundiers. But…

I missed Rayne. I wished she were here with me, supporting me as I took this powldron. She was angry with me for not telling her about Horesk, and I didn't blame her. While I didn't lie, I omitted the truth.

When she reeled away from me in horror, I was dragged right back to the munette my father told me he might provide a roof over my head but not to expect anything further. He pushed me away, a youngling of only six cycles. I lost my mother and then I lost my father.

So, when Horesk insisted it was time to dolce Laylee, I took off after him. I could come back to Rayne after ensuring the pup was safe. We would talk. I would explain.

But after making sure he didn't find her, Garek tracked me down. My uncle sent word. It was time.

Rather than chance Rayne rejecting me, I left her.

I was no better than my father. I was no better than Missy's father.

Within munettes of my arrival at the Willen Clan, I realized my mistake. Rayne would not reject me. She loved me.

I was determined to meld with this powldron quickly and return to her.

"Durran?" my uncle said, nudging the powldron toward me.

It felt wonderful in my hands. "Thank you, Uncle."

Fire leaped in the nearby pit, sending ghostly shadows flickering across the walls. I stared down at the beautiful powldron handcrafted from wood lured from an ednest tree then fused with steel and leather. Only a master could craft such a device, and he must first gain permission from the ednest tree to use its wood. Sadly, our masters had all died.

"Wear it with pride, nephew," my uncle said solemnly. His aged face softened. "As I have worn it with pride and honor myself. Many generations have taken this powldron, melded with it until they became one. It has served me well, gifting me with strength when I was weak and guidance when I was in great need."

I needed guidance.

Rayne.

Despite the wonder of this munette, I could only think of her. My heart ached for her, my arms were empty without her nestled within them, and my body only wished to stand by her side.

Did she think I threw her away like Missy's father?

I would go to her as soon as I could. Would she consider moving to this clan to be with me? It was asking a lot but we…

We loved each other.

Love was more important than anything else.

My uncle jerked his chin forward, urging me to place the powldron on my shoulder. His tail swept solemnly behind him, back and forth.

This was the true test. Would I fail it like I had my father? Missy and I had so much in common. Her father chose not to include her in his life like Horesk did with me. If I were given a chance—a second chance—with Rayne, I would step forward to be the father Missy lacked, should she choose to include me in her life. I wanted to be there for her as she grew, to give her guidance, to scowl at any male who asked to court her, and to figure out how to make a crown braid with her hair.

I stared down at the powldron. All my life I equated this moment with true acceptance, not realizing it must come from within me and not from anyone or anything else.

No one could say I wasn't worthy but me, and I was done with dragging myself to the ground. Tired of feeling I wasn't enough.

Rayne thought I was enough, and I couldn't ask for anything more than that.

With a nod to my uncle and the elder officiating this ceremony, I lifted the powldron and laid it on my shoulder.

I stepped out of the small domit and onto the wooden walkway with my uncle at my side.

His face wreathed with smiles, he hurried forward to speak with those waiting.

"It is done," he said, turning to gesture to me. "Welcome your new warlord."

Stomps and grunts rang out, filling the forest with happiness. Overhead, the trundier herd screeched, adding their voices to the cheering Ferlaern.

After the roar quieted, I stepped up beside my uncle. "Thank you. I welcome the chance to lead but also the chance to provide for this clan. May the future treat us all kindly."

More stomps and grunts greeted my words, and my uncle slapped my shoulder. Had he met the Earthlings?

A swooping sound overhead was followed by a screech and the calling command of a Ferlaern. Was someone flying in close? Why not use the landing platform?

The Willen Clan trundiers squawked in their nests, and I didn't blame them. Their hatchlings were vulnerable. I wanted to run to them, reassure them things would be all right, but they had their own trainer, and this was not my role in this clan.

For a munette, I missed the simplicity of my former life.

The trundier hovered above the canopy, and I stilled when a voice called out.

"Durran!" It sounded just like Rayne.

How was this possible?

My two hearts beat in harmony, telling me my maelstrom mate was nearby. I tipped my head back but couldn't see her through the thick vegetation.

"Durran!"

"I'm here," I called, and the clansmales and few females whispered, speculating about what this might mean.

"I'm coming down," Rayne yelled. "I hope you're good at catching eager Earthling females."

23

Rayne

I'd never repelled off anything, let alone a giant hornet holding position above trees that had to be two hundred feet tall.

A slight exaggeration, but still.

"I'm coming down, and I'm claiming my maelstrom male," I yelled, hoping he'd hear. Hoping I wasn't making an absolute fool of myself.

Narcial cackled and slapped my back hard enough the wind was nearly knocked from me.

Gasping and sucking in air, I latched onto the vine she'd dangled over the side of her trundier, hooked to the creature's spike.

Crap. Could I do this? It was an awfully long way down.

Take a chance or you'll never know what you're missing. That was my new motto.

I closed my eyes for a second and made a wish. Lots of wishes, actually. Then I slipped over the side of Narcial's trundier and dangled in the air while clutching the vine.

At my nod, Narcial lowered me down until my feet

brushed the top of the canopy. I looked down. Shouldn't have looked down. Crap, crap, crap.

I dropped farther, and soon; I was engulfed in leaves. I passed a nest with a startled trundier who might've squawked or challenged me if he or she wasn't so stunned. A cute, tiny baby pup poked its head around its parent and watched me with equally wide eyes as I was lowered past the nest. Ha ha. If I weren't scared shitless about what might happen next, I'd laugh.

Laughter could come later.

Somehow, Narcial hit this right, which could be due to her elder status, her skill with her trundier, or plain old luck. My feet thudded on a wide platform, and a hush descended over the numerous Ferlaern gathered like I'd parachuted into a formal ceremony.

My eyes were only for him—Durran who now wore a powldron on his left shoulder. I didn't know much about them, but the honor of wearing one was clear.

Would a Ferlaern warlord want me?

I was a single mom rejected by her college boyfriend; a slightly overweight woman who had a heart bigger than I should.

It beat only for Durran.

He watched me, his mouth ajar. That was cute. And friendly. It soothed my unease and lent me enough confidence to straighten my dress and stride through the parting Ferlaern.

I walked right up to him.

"Durran," I said.

"Rayne," he breathed.

"You left before I had a chance to tell you I don't care who your father is or if you chose not to share it. I want you forever. I love you."

He tugged me against his chest and wrapped his arms

around me while the Ferlaern grunted and stomped their feet.

"I'm sorry I didn't tell you. Sorry I left without finding you and bringing you with me."

"It's okay as long as…"

"As what?"

"You damn well better want me," I said, my words muffled against his chest. My eyes stung and I wasn't sure if I was going to burst into laughter or bawl.

His arms tightened around me. "Oh, I want you mate."

"Just mate, huh?" I said, leaning back with a smile.

"*Maelstrom* mate," he said. "You're mine for always."

If I didn't need to return to Missy, I would've spent a month in bed with Durran. But my daughter needed me and, well, we needed her. Both of us, not just me.

We flew to the Suthen Clan on Jorlorn, though our trip was merely a visit. Now that Durran was a warlord, he was needed by his clan. We'd pack our things and move to the other valley.

I hated that some things would remain unsettled, but I was confident Garek would discover who was poisoning the trees. And we'd discussed Laylee and would take her with us when we left. The elder of the Willen Clan was kinder than Horesk.

Hell, everyone was kinder than Horesk.

I'd miss Piper, but the clans would soon migrate to the lowlands where we'd spend the summer moons gathered together. We'd visit then, and I couldn't wait to see what the lowlands would be like.

We landed Jorlorn and strolled along the forest path hand-in-hand then took a vine up into the canopy.

When we reached my domit, we were met with Savvy and Missy.

Missy burst into tears and slammed into me, her arms going around my legs.

"What's wrong, honey?" I asked, my gaze seeking Durran.

"We went out to see a trundier pup, the one named… Laylee?" Savvy said, tears in her eyes. "I didn't let her follow. I couldn't. You know, there are…things down there."

Missy keened. "Laylee's gone, Mommy. The mean guy took her to the ground!"

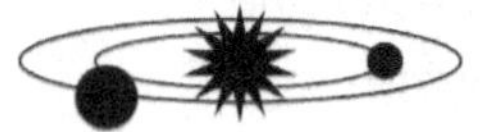

Durran

Anger burned through me. My father rejected me, threw me away, and now he planned to do the same thing with Laylee.

No. Never again.

"I'm going after her," I said.

Rayne's intent gaze met mine. "I'm going with you," she said fiercely.

"Me, too," Missy cried.

Savvy snarled. "If butts are going to be kicked, I'm in."

"It's not safe on the ground," Rayne said to Savvy. "Could you… Would you stay here with Missy?"

Missy wrapped her arms around her mother's leg. "Mommy, I gotta be there for Laylee."

"And I know Laylee wants to see you, too, but she's going to need food when we bring her back. Can you go to the dining domit and get something for her?" Rayne's intent gaze met Savvy's.

Savvy sighed and nodded. "You're right, Rayne. We need to stay here and get things ready for Laylee." She held her hand out to Missy. "Come on. Do you know what to feed a trundier? Because I sure don't. I doubt she's going to eat those gross waffles."

Missy looked up at me, and the tears shimmering in her eyes hit me in the gut like a liscard horn. I'd do just about anything to keep this youngling from feeling pain. "Do you have a lizard, Durran?" Her lower lip trembled. "I'll...try to cut it up and put the chunks on leaves and save both packets, 'cause Laylee's gonna be really hungry."

I stooped down on my knees and held out my arms. She barreled forward and clung, though the top of her head barely cleared my belly. So tiny yet infinitely precious. Would she someday accept me as a father figure in her life?

Rayne's eyes gleamed and even Savvy sniffed while I hugged Missy.

I stroked her hair. "It's going to be...o-kay." That was the word the Earthlings used instead of all right. *Okay.*

"You promise?" Missy said against my chest, and my arms tightened around her. How could I keep her safe for the rest of her life?

"I do. It will be okay." I gulped and my eyes stung. Ferlaern didn't cry; our eyes did not produce water like an Earthling. "As for a lizard, I think instead, Laylee might be interested in fruits and vegetables, which you can get at the dining domit. Would you take a few baskets there and fill them up? Meet us at the nest." I stood, and Missy leaned against me, wiping her eyes.

We left them, and I truly wanted Rayne to remain up here where she was safe. But I knew Rayne wanted— needed—to be with me to see this through. A vine took us to the ground, and we stumbled into Crall.

His gaze flicked between me and Rayne before returning to my powldron. "You? A clan warlord?"

I put my arm around Rayne. "A clan warlord with a maelstrom mate."

Crall's face fell as he took in the symbol on my opposite shoulder. He sneered at Rayne. "If you get bored, you know where to find me."

"That's never happening," Rayne said fiercely.

Crall huffed and stomped over to a vine. He was soon swept up to the canopy.

I held Rayne a munette before we parted.

"Jerk. I'll be glad never to see him again," Rayne said.

She would when the clans gathered but I would speak with Crall before we met up. He'd leave her alone or feel my wrath.

"Where do you think Horesk took Laylee?" Rayne asked, looking around. "I thought," she gulped, "that he'd toss her over the side of the nest, but Missy said he brought her here."

"I don't know." If he took Laylee, he wanted to ensure I couldn't intervene. "But…"

No. He wouldn't, would he?

I had to find out, Taking Rayne's hand, I strode forward, weaving along the path that wound toward the back of this forest. When we emerged from the trees, I sought tracks in the open area overgrown with grass. Few Ferlaern came here and if I found evidence…

There. A fresh footprint in the soft soil.

I held my hand up and tapped my lips. Rayne nodded, indicating she understood we needed to be silent.

Since she didn't have a weapon, I handed her a knife. She may not know how to use it, but it would provide a bit of defense.

We took the path switch backing up the side of the cliff. I hadn't been here for many cycles, not since my heart was ripped from my chest as I watched my mother fall.

Leave it to Horesk to bring Laylee here to dispose of.

He wouldn't do it humanely. Cruelty to me and the defenseless creature was his intent.

Urgency fed my steps as I followed the footprints up the winding path. At the top, I paused to catch my breath within the tree line. Then I crept forward across the open, massive slab of pale blue ledge that covered the top of the mountain.

Rayne's hand tightened on my shirt and a soft whimper slipped from her mouth.

Horesk stood on the edge of the cliff holding the trundier pup above his head. Dolcing was a cruel practice. I'd advocated many times to do away with it, but my father never listened. A pup dying on its own was one thing, but to purposefully kill one? I would no longer stand back and allow him to do this.

I rushed forward, my footsteps light on the stone.

"Stop," I cried, and Horesk froze.

He turned and his tusks gleamed in a cruel smile. "Looking for this?" he asked, waving the keening pup toward me.

"Put her down. Leave her alone." I tripped over something and looked down to find Horesk's pack lying on the smooth surface.

"She needs to be dolced," he snarled. "You didn't do as I demanded."

"You no longer command me."

He drew himself up stiffly. "I am the senior elder of this clan."

It was no longer my clan, but I was not here to make announcements.

"This isn't dolcing," I said. "It's you being a sick bastard."

He cackled and backed closer to the edge. Beyond him, a steep drop-off awaited, the walls of the cliff were steep and jagged with sharp stones. Boulders waited at the bottom for any unfortunate soul who fell.

Like my mother. Remembering ripped me apart all over again. If only I'd been able to save her.

Shoving aside my grief, I stomped over to Horesk. "Mother died here. You brought this hatchling to this specific location despite knowing I care for her, to throw her off. Why? You've spent your life showing I'm nothing to you. Do you need to compound your miserable life by harming an innocent?"

"Innocence has nothing to do with it."

Rayne crept over and stopped beside me, taking my hand, and squeezing it. "Give me the pup," she said. "We'll take care of it."

"That's the problem," Horesk said. "You weren't taking care of it. It should've been dolced sunslices ago."

"It's growing stronger," I said, trying to reason with him. "It'll fly as well as the other trundiers."

A sly look took over Horesk's face. "But you like this one."

I was right. He would kill it in front of me just to make me suffer.

Laylee bleated, her wings flapping as she strained to reach us.

"Where did you get that?" Horesk's gaze focused on my powldron.

I sighed with disgust. Why did this male's opinion still matter to me? "Where they always come from. The warlord offered it to me."

"My brother gave it to you?"

"You sound shocked. Even you knew it was inevitable." I hoped to wait longer before taking over the role but now I welcomed it. In *my* clan, no trundier pup would be dolced. I strode closer and tipped my head to my powldron. "This would've been yours, but you threw it away just like you did me."

"But… But…" Horesk reeled away from me. His foot caught on a root projecting through a crack in the ledge. One of his arms spiraled, and the trundier pup screeched as it was wrenched around.

Rayne ran forward and snatched Laylee from Horesk. She backed away, clutching the pup to her chest.

Horesk caught his footing and snarled. He started toward her with his hands raised, but a gust of wind swept down from the mountains, filled with frigid air. It blasted my back, pushing me forward. Rayne shuddered and sheltered the pup in her arms.

When the wind hit Horesk, he was shoved backward.

His arms flew out to grab onto something but found only air. With a hoarse cry, he tumbled off the cliff.

I leaped forward to help him, but it was too late.

As he dropped away, his eyes met mine. Did I see a hint of remorse there? It didn't appear so, and I was wrong to believe I did.

He was gone.

A long silence was followed by a gut-wrenching thud.

My knees jerked, and my hands sagged to my sides.

"Durran," Rayne choked out. She wiggled Laylee onto one hip and put her other arm around me, leaning her head against my arm. "I'm so sorry. Your father."

I kissed the top of her head and turning, wrapped her up in my arms. "He stopped being a father to me many cycles ago."

"Still." She pressed her cheek against my chest, and I held her as the sun slowly sunk toward the horizon.

I didn't know how I felt. Loss? No. Sorrow? Not even that.

Emptiness. Yes, that was it. As if a tiny piece of me was wrenched away.

When it started to get dark, it was time to leave. I didn't dare risk the forest at night with the duskhorde in the area.

"What will happen to Horesk?" Rayne asked, snuggling Laylee. The creature clung to her; her little wings tucked tight to her back.

"Garek will send someone to collect the body," I said, my voice completely devoid of emotion. "As he was an elder, we'll hold an honorable ceremony for him."

But an era ended with his death.

We picked up his bag as we passed it, and I stopped to open it. Why haul something this heavy up a cliff when he only intended a dolcing?

Horror filled me when I stared down at the contents inside. "Frylar weed."

"What?" Rayne moved in close to peer into the bag. Her dismayed gaze met mine. "Do you think…?"

I shook my head. I still hadn't processed what happened to my father and now…

"Why?" I choked out. I whirled and stomped to the cliff and despite my worry about being discovered by the duskhorde, I shouted the word. "Why?"

Rayne wrapped her arms around me from behind and carefully tugged me backward, away from the edge.

I waited there longer than I should, until the sun winked out on the horizon, but I still had no answer.

"He was destroying our way of life," Rayne said in a low, thready voice as we hurried down the path. "Why would he do something like that?"

Perhaps I did have an answer. "Remember when he

fumed about the Earthlings bringing changes? That our traditions and culture would be cursed if we didn't set you aside."

"He was bringing about a curse himself, ensuring he'd have something to point to when he brought it up again. He intended to blame us for the death of the trees."

I long since lost any affection for my father but this… "How could he do it?" I still didn't understand. He'd destroy what he worried others would change.

Rayne took my hand and squeezed it. "He was a bitter, old male, unhappy with everything."

I dropped the bag, determined to leave it where it fell. Leave Horesk at the base of the cliff, too. He could've killed us all. As it was, we would struggle to save the trees.

Then I tugged her close. Kissed her.

"Rayne," I whispered.

"I'm here for you, Durran," she said softly.

And that was all I needed.

Durran

A Moon Later

"Karaoke tonight?" Rayne asked with a hopeful smile. We lounged on the sofa in the warlord's domit up in the canopy of the Willen Clan's village.

Garek retrieved Horesk's body, and the elder was given a funeral like any other. There was no honor in what he did, and he took his shame to the grave with him.

Thankfully, Narcial knew a cure for the poison left behind by the frylar weed, and the trees were improving.

We packed our possessions, said goodbye to our friends and reminded them we'd see them in a few moons in the lowlands, then Rayne, Missy, Jorlorn, Teddy, Laylee, and me moved to the Willen Clan, where we were made welcome.

I had a family, something I never dreamed possible.

"Karaoke?" I asked, pretending I had no idea what Rayne spoke of. I still had Narcial's notes and… I'd been practicing, but maybe something like this should be a surprise?

"Yes," Rayne said with a smile. "Karaoke. I've mentioned it a billion times. I talked a few of your warriors into hiring a fluffball band, and some of the guys even said they'd sing. But you know that, too, as I've said it a billion times as well." She poked my side, and it tickled.

I, of course, needed to get revenge for this slight. Grinning, I urged her down onto the cushions and loomed over her, sliding my fingers beneath her shirt to tease her skin.

Her laughter burst free as she writhed beneath me. Soon, laughter turned serious, and I captured her mouth with my own.

"Hey, it's time to go feed Laylee, Mommy," Missy said. I looked up to find her peering at us over the back of the sofa. "You too, Durran—I mean, Dad."

Before we moved in together, Rayne and I explained we were going to be a family. Missy rushed up to me and wrapped her arms around my leg.

"Does this mean you'll learn to braid my hair?" she asked, tipping her head back to look up at me.

"Even if you want a crown."

"And you'll tuck me in at night and tell me a story?"

"I will," I said solemnly.

She tilted her head. "Do you like to play tea?"

I looked to Rayne who beamed at both of us.

"Tea?" I said, half gulping.

"Yeah, tea. With my dolls," Missy said. "I make tea and my dolls drink it. You gotta drink it instead, okay?"

"I'd be happy to." Anything to see a smile on this sweet child's face.

"Yay." She hugged me again then frowned. "If you're gonna be my dad, shouldn't I call you Daddy?"

I placed a fist against my chest and my eyes stung

again. No tears. Ferlaerns didn't produce tears. "I'd be honored."

And now we were a family.

"We need to leave," Missy said again. "Laylee's waiting for us."

Rayne and I got up and we left the domit, taking the walkways to the hatchling grounds. Most of the hatchlings had bonded with Ferlaerns, though Laylee had yet to choose anyone.

We set her up in an open nest, as there was no need to hide her. Under the kind care of the trundier trainer, she was growing huge and strong. I expected her to take her first test flight soon.

We arrived at her nest, and the pup peered over the side and chirped at us in happiness.

I handed Missy a pouch of food, and she clambered up the branch to feed and play with the hatchling. Rayne and I sat on a bench to wait.

"Laylee," Missy cried, and we looked in that direction. "Hey, Daddy, I… I'm bonding with her!"

Rayne looked up at me with lifted eyebrows. "Is that possible?"

"She's the right age." I called out to my…daughter. She *was* my daughter, of my heart if not my seed. Families were formed by more than blood. "They both are."

"Missy's too young," Rayne said, her voice tight.

"We'll work with her. She'll be okay." I pulled my maelstrom mate up onto my lap and wrapped my arms around her. "She's a Ferlaern now. You both are. This is our tradition."

"We are, aren't we?" she said with joy. "Thank you."

"For what?"

"For loving us, for giving us a home, and for being so special."

I rested my forehead against hers. "I should be thanking you, mate, for the same. Thank you for coming into my life and giving my two hearts a home."

Life wasn't complete without karaoke, or so I was told. After Rayne and Missy left to get things ready for tonight, I paced our domit, nearly wearing a hole in the floor.

Could I do this? I was the clan's warlord. They expected me to always act in a leaderlike manner.

Singing… I just wasn't sure. But I did want to see Rayne smile.

I strolled to the community domit, my steps slowing as I got closer. Music boomed from the building, and laughter rang out.

This was supposed to be fun. No one would stare at me. I wouldn't feel uncomfortable.

Sure.

Bruge, the warlord of the Nulet Clan, met me at the entrance. "You decided to show, did you?" he said with a deep laugh.

"You were expecting me?"

"Well, your mate said something about how you might be stopping by to sing," Bruge said. "This, I had to see."

"It isn't funny," I said easily. I slapped his shoulder as Earthlings did and tried not to grin when he winced. "I'm going to sing with my maelstrom mate."

"For that, I envy you." He grunted and hurried to explain. "Not Rayne, that is, but being fully bonded with a female. I hoped…" He peered around me like he expected someone else to show up.

"Hoped what?"

"When you were at the Suthen Clan, did you talk

much with Alexa?"

"Alexa?" I leaned around Bruge, trying to see inside. I needed to determine what would be expected of me tonight.

"Yes, Alexa. She has two younglings. They're three cycles old."

"I know Alexa, yes." She asked about Bruge. Was there something between them? I wondered if things would develop between them when the clans drew together in the lowlands. If Bruge was interested in Alexa, he'd have competition. Should I tell him?

"Did she…mention me?" he asked, strain coming through in his voice.

Oh, I could tease him about this. "Maybe." I scratched my head. "I'm not sure."

Bruge growled. He pulled one of his weapon's straps to the side, showing off skin. "What do you think of this?"

I leaned in close, squinting. "Looks like a maelstrom mark to me."

"It's been there since I met her."

Ah. "Why are you here then, and not at the Suthen Clan courting your mate?"

"I had trouble in my clan and had to deal with that first." He stiffened. "But now…"

"What?"

"What do Earthlings think about abduction?"

"What do you mean?" I half-shouted. Alexa might not be in my clan any longer, but my protection extended to her.

The music slowed inside, then grunts and stomps erupted as Ferlaerns cheered.

Bruge ran his fingers through his thick hair. "When I tried to talk to her, she ignored me."

"Maybe you weren't persuasive enough."

"Yes! That was my thought. Since then, I've been speculating about how best to handle this. Abducting her and taking her to an oasis where I can show her that she's mine might be the best way to handle this."

"I'm not sure about that, Bruge." Where had he gotten that idea?

"You think not?" Bruge frowned. "I guess I could choose another way to win her. By the time she arrives in the lowlands, I should have a plan."

"I wish you luck."

"Thanks."

Shaking my head, I brushed past him, needing to see my own maelstrom mate. When the leader of the band saw me, the creature gave me a nod.

Weaving around laughing Ferlaern, I worked my way to a table near the stage. Fuck, a stage? Rayne didn't notice me until I stood in front of her.

"You came," she exclaimed, leaping off her seat and into my arms. She buried her face in my neck. "You smell good." She licked my ear, making me shiver. "Taste good, too. If you want..." Peering over her shoulder, she sought our daughter. "We could take Missy back, put her to bed, then put ourselves to bed."

"Soon, mate," I said. "I have something I need to do first."

She leaned back in my arms. "What is it?"

The music started and she frowned. "Aw, that's my favorite song. I wonder who's going to sing it?"

"We are."

Her eyes widened. "Really?"

"Really."

I lowered her to her feet then led her up onto the stage. Then I got down on my knees and did my best to croon about feeling the love tonight.

I was no lion, and I couldn't sing. But I sure did love this female, and that had to come through in my voice.

Rayne's true, strong voice joined in, singing her part, sharing that she was a wide-eyed wanderer, that our hearts beat in time together.

It was wondrous, pure, and my eyes stung all over again.

I wasn't crying. Ferlaern never cried.

Or did they?

I hope you enjoyed Rayne & Durran's story!
Would you like to read a bonus epilogue?
Durran's still in the courting mood, and
he's about to give Rayne a pedicure.
It's yours when you sign up
for my newsletter.
Sign me up!

If you'd like to read Chapter 1 of *Seduced by an Alien Warlord*,
Book 3 in the Fated Mates of the Ferlaern Warriors Series,
turn the page!

If you enjoyed Durran & Rayne's story,
would you leave a review?
It would mean so much to me!
You can leave your review on Amazon.

About the Author

Ava Ross fell for men with unusual features when she first watched Star Wars, where alien creatures have gone mainstream. She lives in New England with her husband (who is sadly not an alien, though he is still cute in his own way), her kids, and a few assorted pets.

Skoar

a Brides of Driegon novella

FATED MATES OF THE FERLAERN WARRIORS

Enticed by an Alien Warlord

Tamed by an Alien Warlord

Seduced by an Alien Warlord

Tempted by an Alien Warlord

You can find my books on Amazon.

SEDUCED BY AN ALIEN
WARLORD

He's a proud alien warlord.
She's a single mom hoping to find love again.
When their worlds collide, sparks fly.

Bruge: I'm a serious warlord, not a youngling warrior in need a mate. Ensuring the duskhorde don't kill us and that the clan gathering runs smoothly is enough to keep me busy. Court an Earthling female? Perhaps later. But when I meet Alexa, my second heart starts beating, proving she's my maelstrom mate. Now I want her, and the best way to claim her is with an ancient Ferlaern tradition: abduction and seduction. If only my entire village would stop trying to help make it happen.

Alexa: I've crushed on Bruge for a while. He's grumpy, gruff, and he has interesting social skills. What's not to like? A widow raising three-year-old twin boys, I still have room in my life for romance. But whenever Bruge and I get close, we either wind up in trouble or we're interrupted. Even better? His warriors follow us around snickering. Our relationship is going nowhere fast, but I'm not giving up, because there's more than one way to seduce an alien warlord.

Turn the page to read Chapter 1...

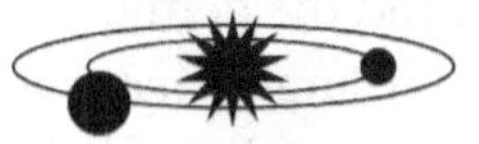

Chapter 1
BRUGE

Our Ferlaern Clans would gather together in the lowlands over the next few sunslices, and while I looked forward to visiting with each individual, there was one Earthling female I was eager to see most of all.

Alexa.

I finished the final touches on the domit I'd present to her when she arrived. Had I done too much? She was worthy of my best efforts, but Earthlings were complicated.

Too damn confusing.

It was hard to know what might offend her. From the short time I interacted with her, I could tell she was assertive and independent. She wouldn't enjoy a heavy hand.

As a female worthy of a clan warlord, perhaps she wished to finish the construction of her own domit? Many Ferlaern females do.

Glancing around the interior one last time, I contemplated what else I could do to make her feel welcome. I heard Earthling females enjoyed flowers but few grew on this region of the plain. I doubted she'd enjoy a bouquet of drended stems as they were apt to bite if someone came close. And the pularn blossoms would take up half a room. Perhaps I could squeeze a few truedrops into the small vegetable garden behind the domit.

This unit was a bit larger than most, but she had two younglings. Her sons would need their own space. The central portion contained a living area, and I crafted two attached bedrooms, one for her and the other for her younglings.

Wait. What if I—

The flap of winged trundiers made my two hearts skip several beats. Turning, I pushed aside the door flap and stepped outside, my gaze seeking the sky. Was Alexa arriving?

From the munette I met her, she called to me. I ached to run my fingers through her hair the color of ripened worthisk grains. To touch her curvy form. When she watched me with her dark blue eyes stormier than the river cutting through the plain behind our village, my second heart seized.

She was my fated maelstrom mate. Finding the symbol on my shoulder only confirmed what I already knew. My second heart came to life the munette I saw her.

Now to convince her she was mine.

"They are here," my mother said, walking up beside me. A sneer filled her bronze face, creasing her segmented skin. A breeze caught her lavender hair, making the black strands glisten. "Earthings." She spat. "You heard what happened with Durran, did you not?"

"Yes," I said, striving for patience. "He told me himself." And she'd told me at least five times.

"H left the Suthen Clan."

"His uncle passed on his powldron." I ran my fingers across my own powldron I'd bonded with eight cycles ago, before my father died.

"He left because of *her*."

"Not completely. His father…" I growled, not wishing to go through this again. My mother did not like the Earthlings, and nothing would change that.

"I, for one, will not be here to greet them," she said with a huff. She spun on her heel and stalked toward the opposite side of the village.

I pushed my irritation with her aside. Now was for greeting Alexa.

A trundier screeched overhead as a large flight of them circled. Recognizing the beasts from the Osten Clan, my excitement waned. The mighty winged creatures dropped to the ground beyond the fence.

My friend, Zetar, slid off his beast and gave it a long pat before striding over to where I remained outside Alexa's domit. I'd crafted it from the most attractive wuldra husks, suspecting a female's heart might take joy in living within something pretty. The plant's broad leaves were easily woven into a tight mesh, making them impervious to water and…

And they…*spanked*. No, that was not the correct word. They *sparkled*.

Warriors from Zetar's Clan strode past us, heading toward the wuldra trees growing along the riverbank. They'd harvest leaves to encase their own, skeletal domits. Soon, our village would come alive again.

Each cycle, our clans spent the hot summer months in domits hidden deep within the mountain valleys. There, we bonded with trundier hatchlings and began their training. During the relatively cooler winter months, we migrated to the lowlands. Here, we hunted the warslettes, cleaning and drying their meat to enjoy while living in the mountains. Hunting was scarce in the hills, much of the creatures consumed by the ferocious liscards.

"You won't believe what I saw not far from here," Zetar said grimly. His feet scuffed the dry soil and the wind swept it up and carried it across the endless plain. He turned his squinted gaze to the deep golden, wavering grasses. "A large tribe of duskhorde are crossing the northern plain, heading toward our mountain valleys."

I lifted a hand toward my second-in-command, Frelz, and he strode over, his heavy gaze passing between us.

"You should hear this," I said, nudging my head to Zetar, who repeated what he saw.

"Do you think they hope to take over our summer domits in the mountains?" Frelz asked. "It makes no sense."

"Of what use are our domits without trundiers?" Zetar wisely asked. "This is why we choose to live there."

"And the trundiers travel with us," I said. Only a few unbonded beasts remained in the mountains. They would resist any dusklen who tried to take up residence in the trees.

I didn't like this, though I couldn't point to what made unease grind through me like a jagged blade. Skirmishes with the duskhorde were relatively uncommon, so them passing across the plain even in a large group could be ignored unless they approached our winter village. But heading into the mountains? They rarely traveled there other than in small packs to raid eggs and hatchlings, and the remaining mature adult trundiers could protect itself from the horde.

"We could speculate for sunslices and not understand why they do anything," I finally said.

Frelz raked his fingers through his black hair shot through with only a few strands of purple. I'd inherited more of lavender coloring from my mother and had only a few bands of black. My height and deeper bronze skin came from my father. "They drove a sizeable herd of warslette."

Interesting. The herds were plentiful in the lowlands. I wasn't necessarily worried about the duskhorde claiming what they needed. We all had to eat, and I'd rather the duskhorde consume warslette than us.

"Perhaps they plan to take the narrow passage through the far edge of the mountains," I said. "I heard other dusklen tribes liv in the valleys beyond." Concern filled me, keeping me unsettled. I nodded to Frelz who likely knew what I was thinking already. "Wing after them. Follow them to see what they do, but don't let them know you watch. Once you've determine their plan, report back. By then, the rest of the clans will have arrived and we can discuss how best to handle this."

"Very well." Frelz pressed his fist against his chest. He spun and strode toward the trundier flock. His mounted soon winged into the sky, and I watched until they merged with the horizon.

"The Earthling females will be here soon," Zetar said, rocking on his heels. He flashed his tusks in irritation.

"You as well?" I said.

"Not all of them." Zetar scowled. "Just one."

"Which one in particular?"

Zetar shook his head. "It does not matter."

Yet here he was, letting one irritate him. Which female had caught his eye?

"Alexa will be with them," I said. Even speaking her name made my pulse surge.

Zetar had seen my matebond symbol. He knew my

thoughts about this particular female. So did Durran. I told him of my interest in Alexa when I visited his clan many sunslices ago. If only I'd seen her then, but when I looked for her, I couldn't find her. Someone said she was in the community domit, singing, and as much as I ached to hear her lilting voice in song, the demands of my clan needed to come first.

They should all the time. Why couldn't I stop thinking about her, doing things for her? My father had been the unofficial lead warlord when the clans gathered on the plain. I had stepped into this role when his powldron fused to my shoulder. There would not be time this cycle to court a female.

"Will you claim Alexa?" Zetar asked.

I snorted. "The true question is, will she be willing to be claimed?"

"She has younglings. They keep her busy." He scratched the back of his neck. "They will take up much of her time."

"She cannot be too busy for mating, I don't believe. Her younglings are a gift."

Zetar snorted. "Have you interacted with them? I have, and they are more than one handful. At least three or four."

"I welcome the task of taming them."

"As well as Alexa," Zetar said with a flash of his tusks. "How do you plan to win her? Will you use the standard courtship rituals or experiment with those of the Earthlings?" He scowled again. "Their expectations are too steep."

Ah, so that's how this was. Had he tried to court one of the Earthlings already?

"I thought I might try one of our ancient traditions," I said.

"Such as?"

My lips curved up. "Abduction and seduction."

You can find Seduced by an Alien Warlord on Amazon.